OBAKE

GHOST STORIES IN HAWAI'I

BY GLEN GRANT

MUTUAL PUBLISHING

I

Design
Michael Horton Design

Illustrations
Ross Yamanaka

Fifth Printing January 1996
5 6 7 8 9

Mutual Publishing
1127 11th Avenue, Mezz. B
Honolulu, Hawaii 96716
Ph: (808) 732-1709
Fax: (808) 734-4094
Email: mutual@lava.net

Printed in Australia

Table of Contents

PREFACE

Obake in Hawai'i: The Path of a Storyteller into Undiscovered Country

"Do ghosts really exist?"

It is a question I have been asked a thousand times. For those who believe that they have made spirit contact, such a question is irrelevant. Of course the dead return from their graves—we've seen their apparitions, heard their disembodied voices, or felt their chilling presence on a cold, lonely night. For those from many non-Western cultures, communication with the "other world" is ingrained in daily life. The 'aumakua, or ancestral spirits of the Native Hawaiian community, are real for those who seek their consultation or guidance. The thousands of Chinese in Hawaii who annually visit the graves of their ancestors during the Ch'ing Ming festival know that the spirits of their loved ones are strengthened through the nourishment offered at the gravesite. For those who revere their dead, there is no question that the human personality survives beyond the grave and can influence the living.

For the skeptic who has been taught that the material world is the limit of their knowledge, the idea of ephemeral beings moving objects or haunting houses seems highly implausible. Ghosts are to the materialists, in the immortal words of

Ebenezer Scrooge, "humbug." There is no evidence of spirit return that will satisfy these skeptics, short of shaking hands with an apparition. Still, even the most die-hard materialist can enjoy a ghost story as folklore that reflects the marvelous power of the human imagination to conjure up phantoms, demons, monsters or poltergeists.

There is another group of inquirers for whom the issue of whether things actually do go bump in the night remains an open-ended proposition. These are people who have never had a first-hand experience with spirit communication, yet who believe in its possibility. Never having seen a ghost, yet open to their possible existence, these spirit-seekers love to hear about the experiences of others, perhaps even contemplating their own visit to a cemetery on a black, moonless evening or sleeping overnight in a haunted house. For these inquirers, the reality of the supernatural will remain forever unanswered, until that voice reaches across the gulf of death to whisper in their ear, "Yes, we do exist."

Tactfully, for the last twenty-five years that I've collected the ghost stories of Hawaii, I have avoided answering this most interesting question—not necessarily because I don't have an answer, but because ultimately no response will be satisfactory. The spirit-seer doesn't ask; the skeptic isn't going to accept a "yes" without scientifically tested data; the ghost-seeker wants an apparition to materialize so that their faith can be confirmed. Since I cannot produce the evidence or phantom, I have no resolution to a question that has haunted the human race since we first buried our dead, wondering where they had gone, and where would we follow.

However, I can share the stories that I have been privileged to hear from thousands of sources in the Hawaiian Islands—written and oral—which have taught me how the spirits of the dead communicate with the living. This ghost storytelling began early in my life, for, even as a child, I had been greatly influenced by the purportedly true tales of apparitions which my father used to tell around the dinner table. He always prefaced his stories by assuring me that, "I swear on a stack of Bibles it happened," an affirmation of truthfulness which I soon learned to emulate with my friends as I later retold the tales around the campfire. As a teenager, I had earned the reputation for being the "ghost guy," absorbing every book on the subject by Hans Holzer and repeating ad nauseam every allegedly true story I heard. Oddly enough, I was never interested in the fictional tales of the supernatural. Stephen King or Clive Barker-type literature strikes me as ludicrous, although I have sometimes been likened to them in my macabre interests. Recognizing early in my writing and storytelling career, however, that I really have no imagination, I soon depended upon simply retelling as matter-as-factly as possible the incredible occurrences which others had experienced.

When I arrived in Honolulu in 1970 to attend the University of Hawaii as a graduate student, I had no idea that the Islands were alive with ghosts. After one semester working in Japanese American studies with Dr. Dennis M. Ogawa, I realized that nearly every student in the class had family ghost stories or even personal experiences with the supernatural. Seeking more island stories in the library, I was disappointed to discover that, although many scholars had collected and recorded myths and legends from ancient Hawaiian civilization, few had ever studied the modern lore of Hawaii. Studies of contemporary supernatural contact was limited to a few scholarly articles and newspaper accounts of local hauntings which occasionally were reported around the Halloween season. How had such an incredibly rich aspect of the Islands' oral traditions been overlooked?

Thus my collection began, working with fellow students, digging into the newspaper files, talking with kupuna, the elders, and even visiting such notable sites as Morgan's Corner in the dead of night. Occasionally, former students, now public school teachers, would invite me to share the stories with their class. The stories which had been earlier confined to written records were then transformed into retold tales, exciting interest and awe in students of all ages. The collection expanded as members of the audience would approach me after the presentation to share their own stories of encounters with ghosts.

Many colleagues urged me to publish these island stories in an anthology. Initially, I was hesitant to simply retell the story as I had heard it—over the years often the name of the original source of the tale had been lost or forgotten. I certainly didn't want to misrepresent the original occurrence while promoting the story as "factual." Most importantly, I didn't want to insult any of the spirits who appeared in the stories. "The spirits attach themselves to the storyteller," I was often told by those elders in the community far wiser than I. And, if they don't appreciate the way they are being described, then bachi, "bad luck," would be the result. That was a sufficient warning—it was better to wait than to plunge ahead with committing the tales to the written word.

In 1983, my colleague and friend Arnold Hiura, who was at that time the editor of The *Hawaii Herald,* convinced me that an article on Hawaii's Japanese *obake* would be interesting to his readership, many of whom were Japanese Americans. "In Search of Kappa and Mujina: Japanese Obake in Hawaii" was the result; the public response was favorable. The following year, Arnold again encouraged me to contribute a ghost story for the "Halloween" issue. Reluctant to merely repeat stories I had collected in the community, I decided to combine true stories with my own limited imagination. Drawing upon the journal entry-style which had made Bram Stoker's *Dracula* so compelling, I fashioned "Inu-gami: A Case of Dog Spirit Possession." Nothing in the story suggested that it was actually fiction, based upon a few true stories that I had collected in the community.

The reaction of the public to the story was surprising. Dozens of calls came in to the newspaper, readers attempting to identify the victim of the dog possession or the location of the house. Some readers wanted to offer suggestions on how to bless the young victim; others were terribly concerned about my safety following the supposed attack upon me by the supernatural beast. The sensational response caused by the "inu-gami" tale convinced me of the power of these stories to captivate, enthrall and also entertain islanders of all races and backgrounds. In the following ten years, The *Hawaii Herald,* under the editorship of Arnold Hiura and then Karleen Chinen, offered me a creative venue to weave the stories from Hawaii's people in a way to combine fact with fiction.

The stories which are here reprinted from this ten-year effort combine many different styles. All of them are based upon stories that I've heard or investigated, combined with historical settings, fictional names or traditional Japanese *obake* hauntings. "The Obake-Neko of Kaimuki," for example, is based upon a supernatural creature familiar to Japanese film buffs—the "cat-woman spirit," which was a favorite theme in the old "obake" movies. The stories in "The Ghosts of a Plantation Camp" are all derived from a wonderful year of monthly meetings with the *kupuna* of Waialua, arranged through the Waialua Community Association, to chronicle the oral traditions of the residents of a multicultural rural community. "Out of the Sea at Mokuleia" is based upon a story shared with me by a 90-year-old *issei* picture bride who, in her native tongue, shared with me what has definitely become one of my favorite orally recited tales. While she made no connection between the ethereal beings seen on a lonely Oahu beach and ancient Hawaiian legends of *mo'o,* or supernatural lizards, the cross-cultural blending of Asian and Polynesian lore was beautifully woven throughout her tale.

"Don't Step on My Grave" is an example of a tale inspired by an actual telephone call that I received one afternoon from a very desperate woman. Like the character in the story, the young caller had inadvertently stepped upon a grave in a Japanese cemetery, after which a series of strange occurrences took place that nearly destroyed her family. Convinced that an *obake* had possessed her, she requested the name of an exorcist who could remove the demon within. I should stress that, while I enjoy listening to everyone's stories and can make some referrals for supernatural counseling, never (NEVER!) call me to exorcise the ghosts from your house or person. Not only don't I have any psychic powers, I'm basically a coward.

Soon after this most interesting phone call had taken place, I found myself spending several freezing months in wintry Tokyo. Having only a scant knowledge of Japanese culture, and lacking any ability to communicate in Nihongo, I spent most of my free time bundled up in my *manshon* (apartment) with the heater turned to overload, practicing my *hiragana* flashcards and consuming every *obake* story I could obtain in English. I had promised Arnold that I would submit my annual story *before* leaving for Japan but, as usual, had missed my deadline. With the tale of the grave-stepping victim still on my mind, I wedded her terror to a traditional nineteenth century story of unrequited love, jealousy and bloody revenge. With my travel notes helping to flesh out the much-needed ambiance of Ginza-shopping and moonlit feudal castles, I was able to complete the story just before the presses were to roll, with Hiura-san preparing to commit *harakiri*. The other story that was based upon my sojourn in Japan, "On the Kwaidan Trail of Lafcadio Hearn," may not seem at first a ghost story. Yet, as I reflect on those incredible series of coincidences that led me to the ashes of that distinguished ghost storyteller, I am convinced that of all the tales herein collected, it is the one that proves to me that the dead can, and do, communicate with the living.

Two tales included in *Obake in Hawaii* are something of a departure from the traditional ghost story, venturing into the genre of *Black Mask*-type detective tales. The origin of Arthur McDougal of the Honolulu International Detective Agency is traced to a real-life private gumshoe in Honolulu, Arthur McDuffie, who was once Chief of Detectives for the Honolulu Police Department. I stumbled into the life of Detective McDuffie as a result of one of my walking tours for *Honolulu TimeWalks*, Honolulu: The Crime Beat. Here was the perfect protagonist not only for my "living history" recreation of the past, but for a series of fictional stories written in the shadows of Dashiell Hammet or Raymond Chandler. Changing the surname so as to liberate him from historical fact, Art McDougal was born, first appearing in the *Honolulu Star-Bulletin*. Once a month, the stories of McDougal walking the mean streets of 1930 Honolulu, encountering a wide range of thugs, molls and wise guys, appeared in the newspaper. When they finally retired "Mac," Karleen Chinen, then the new editor of The *Hawaii Herald*, allowed me to reprise him as long as his new arch-nemesis was otherworldly. "The Kasha of Kaimuki" and "The Calling Ghost of Kipapa" showed that even the most hard-headed private dick can sometimes bite off a little more than he can chew when he faces the *obake* of old Japan. For those of you who enjoy Honolulu-based detective stories, McDougal is presently collaborating with artist Ross Yamanaka to dust off a few of his old cases in an upcoming anthology to be called *Honolulu Crime Beat: The McDougal Tapes*. The last story in this first collection of Hawaii supernatural tales is entitled "Kanashibari: The Choking Ghost." For those of you who have experienced this type of phenomena, the fear of being pressed to your bed while sleeping by some heavy weight that sits upon your chest, crushing the air from your lungs, is very real. Medical doctors have suggested a variety of explanations for the cause of the malady—including psychosomatic dreams, chemical imbalances, excessive tiredness, or a string of other personal disorders. A few years ago, national talk show host, Larry King, had a guest on his radio program who discussed sleeping disorders. Someone called the show claiming he was being choked at night, describing the occurrence with all the details of *kanashibari*. The doctor explained that the sensation is a result of the brain being awake while the body remains asleep—a perfectly natural explanation for the choking sensation. Then, suddenly, the doctor asked the caller if he had seen anyone in the room with him while the pressing took place.

"No," the man answered.

"Why did you ask that?" inquired Mr. King.

"Many times the persons who experience this type of sleeping disorder," the doctor calmly responded, "claim that there is someone in the room with them when the choking occurs. Usually an old woman."

"What's that all about?" probed the radio host.

"We have no idea," was the scientist's terse answer.

He may not have any idea about the deeper mysteries of *kanashibari*, but the countless people in Hawaii who have been pressed, with the face of an elderly woman sometimes hovering but inches from their own, will tell you that it is indeed the "terror that comes in the night." My own investigation into a choking ghost on May 3, 1991, culminating with the assault upon the Australian spiritual medium at one of the University of Hawaii dormitories, is a factual account of how trapped spirits may sometimes cause havoc with the living. In reflection, I've often considered the impact that ghost storytelling may have had in accelerating those strange events. Was it because of the downtown "Haunted Honolulu" walking tours that I had been drawn into the haunting? How was it that so many people connected to the life of the young suicide victim had suddenly taken that tour—"coincidences" that resulted in the spirit's "rescue?"

The ghost stories which you are about to explore will not resolve your own doubts as to "can these bones live again?" They are presented not as proof of spirit communication, but merely as a whetting of the appetite for the mysteries that surround our island home. With the completion of this first series on obake in Hawaii, we will next turn our attention to writing down the stories of other first-hand supernatural experiences in the Islands. These hauntings will go beyond the Japanese traditions to reveal a few of the wondrous occurrences that take place on all of the Hawaiian Islands, among all of our diverse cultures and religions. This next volume should be ready in 1995.

Among the thousands of thank-yous which are required, both among the living and the dead, for the appearance of *Obake in Hawaii,* three are outstanding. Arnold Hiura first encouraged, then pushed, cajoled and finally guided me into creating the supernatural stories that are here presented. He has diligently re-edited them for this current publication. This is the first joint creative effort of our new partnership, which aims to tell the many fascinating stories of Hawaii to the world. Bennett Hymer is a publisher who may on the surface at times seem more interested in the bottom line than the comma, but who has always provided unflagging support and moral encouragement. His faith in the talent of writers, artists and designers has helped make Mutual Publishing an invaluable source for creative storytelling and perpetuating the cultural heritage of the Islands. Jill Staas has in the last two years tirelessly guided Honolulu *TimeWalks,* booking more tours and storytelling sessions than is humanly possible to deliver. Yet, through her constant support and encouragement, believing in the beauty of the stories, she has contributed significantly to the creation of the final product.

Others have assisted in the publication of *Obake in Hawaii,* including Ross Yamanaka and Michael Horton, who recognized that even the best-told ghost story requires an artistic interpretation to haunt the imagination. Michael's creative designs and suggestions have added an aura of professionalism to the final product, while Ross' wood block drawings wonderfully capture the mystical visions contained within the tales. A collaboration has hopefully been born between the artists and the storytellers. No writing project can be completed without the type of support that was offered by Cady Kaneko, Jody Tsutomi and Betsy Kubota. Not only did they diligently assist in the typing and copy editing of *Obake in Hawaii*, they provided just enough groans, "ughs" and "ohs" to convince us that these stories were worth publishing.

To the thousands of people who over the years have shared with me their tales of wonder, I extend my most sincere *mahalo*. Your tales and spiritual experiences are embodied in all my storytelling. Although you may not recognize your individual contribution to this finished product, your stories are alive in the many spirits that are conjured up in the retelling. May you always find my storytelling filled with nothing but respect and love for the mysteries of this world and the next.

And to my mother and father, who never lived long enough in this world to see in print my words of dedication, you filled my young mind with the adventure of ghosts that now consumes my middle passage. From this lonely, lost place among the living, I continue to gaze through the glass darkly, searching for the glimpse of a familiar smile, or is it only the will-o'-the-wisp?

In old Japan, the rakugo, or storyteller, always told ghostly tales on warm, humid summer nights. When a story is truly unsettling, it causes the skin to tingle and the hair to rise, sending shivers down your back. The Japanese call this physical condition *torihada*, or "chickenskin." It is used to "cool off" an audience.

So, dim all the lights in your house, cuddle up beneath a small, glowing lamp and get ready to experience "chickenskin." What you are about to discover may have been fictionalized, but it is based upon a very real truth. Even now, that "truth" may be moving about your own house, gliding as a dark shadow into your closet, waiting for you to slip into slumber. Did you hear that creak in the kitchen? Is the wind blowing unnaturally loud? Are you certain that you don't believe in ghosts?

In Search of Kappa and Mujina: Japanese Obake in Hawaiʻi

The Hawaiian Islands abound with ghosts. There is no district on any island that doesn't have some tale about night marchers, *akualele* or fireballs, *kahuna* magic, legends surrounding magical stones or the fire goddess Pele, vanishing hitchhikers, or other manifestations of the return of the dead. Modern high-rise condominiums smack-dab in Honolulu are still plagued by the spirits of unhappy ancestors whose graves had been disturbed by the construction of the buildings. Highways, bridges and newly erected homes are consecrated to prevent future hauntings. Scratch the surface of any placid rural scene and you might very well stumble into a supernatural world of folk wisdom and lore that reminds you of the ancient days when nature, man, spirit and God were one.

The great majority of urban and rural ghosts found in contemporary Hawaii are Hawaiian in origin. After a thousand years of inhabiting the land, it is only natural that the legends, myths and supernatural perceptions of the Native Hawaiians should form the spiritual bedrock of modern occult occurrences. But Hawaiian spirits are tolerant, and there is also room in the Islands for the supernatural traditions of later immigrants.

The *issei,* those Japanese who immigrated to Hawaii in the decades immediately prior to and following the turn of the century, seemed especially keen in preserving the ghostly heritage of their homeland. Considering the Japanese penchant for *obake,* or "weird things," it is small wonder, then, that in plantation camps and urban districts throughout Hawaii the shadowy images of Meiji-era Japan should have moved across the ethnic phantasmagoria.

A Japanese vampire with a crown of burning candles is seen in Waipahu. Her long, silky black hair drifts up into the air and wraps around the neck of her helpless prey. A samurai sword displayed in a St. Louis Heights home produces a frightening poltergeist, as do a similar pair of swords buried during World War II beneath a fern plant in front of a Buddhist shrine on Maui. An entire village on Kauai seems to go mad in the late 1930s, as issei and nisei women are attacked by the *inu-gami,* the dog spirit. During the annual *O-bon* festival in Haleiwa, a family is reunited with the spirit of a friend who had died ten years before. When the white-haired *baban* finishes her prayer before the family altar with the two soft claps of her hand—look into the *butsudan* and see the notion of spirit and faith.

"Japan possesses more legends than any country in the Western world," writes Richard Dorson, an American folklorist who has extensively studied the folk legends of Japan. Dorson's appraisal of the Japanese imagination is especially applicable in terms of the ghosts and monsters of Japan. The Japanese love for *obake* stories, reflected in the traditional *kabuki* theater, modern film and familiar "talk story," is rarely surpassed by other cultures in terms of openness, acceptance and belief. While a Western mind might scoff at "things that go bump in the night" and the Polynesian might refuse to repeat a ghostly tale for fear that the spirit of the story might be inadvertently conjured up, the Japanese have enjoyed centuries of believing in, and talking about, their ghosts.

On warm summer nights, an *obake* tale cools off the listener by causing shivers to run down the spine. It was believed that if 100 such tales are told at a single sitting, and a candle lit for each one, then the assembled storytellers will see a ghost by midnight.

And what youngster of Japanese ancestry, regardless of genera-
tion, growing up in Hawaii has not been taken by their issei,
nisei or sansei parents to the Japanese cinema to see the horren-
dously deformed face of the dead, of her tormentors, or of the cat
demon transforming itself into a beautiful maiden?

It is only natural to expect, then, that in the rich supernatural
folklore of modern Hawaii there would be an abundance of Japanese *obake* tales commingling with Hawaiian spirits. Indeed,
within the Japanese American home and community, there is an
endless array of such tales and psychic phenomena. But the chal-
lenging question is whether the Japanese ghost has become so
integrated into contemporary Island society that people of other
ethnic backgrounds also see them or talk about them. Like the
Hawaiian spirit that is seen by tourists, Japanese, Haoles, Filipinos or whoever else stumbles into a haunted valley or picks up a
sacred stone, have the Japanese *obake* transcended their ethnic
boundaries and become, in essence, Island property?

Reviewing the scores of tales and phenomena that I have collected over the years, the first inclination is to respond to this
question with a definite "No!" The great majority of Japanese
ghost stories, reflecting district Japanese motifs or themes, seem
to be told and experienced only by people of Japanese ancestry or
those who have lived in a Japanese home or intermarried into a
Japanese family. There seems to be a direct relation between seeing an *obake* and being exposed to Japanese culture. When people
of other nationalities have reported seeing a Japanese spirit, it
has usually been in a Japanese setting. For example, Wako's Japanese Restaurant was the scene of a haunting in the early 1970s.
Patrons of all backgrounds had evidently been served by a ki-
mono-clad waitress who dutifully and silently poured their tea.
Later, they would ask their regular waitress who the special tea-
pourer was—to their shock they discovered that she was the spirit
of a former, unhappy worker who had committed suicide. In this
and numerable other cases, the Japanese *obake* was seen in the
context of a Japanese environment or cultural referent.

The search for a Japanese ghost in Hawaii, seen collectively
by Islanders of all nationalities and in a non-Japanese setting,
leads to some very dark corridors of the folk imagination. The

dilemma is to identify contemporary Island ghosts, seen by a diversity of people wholly independent of Japanese background or environment that has distinct roots in traditional Japanese folklore or mythology. If such an entity could be found, then one could surmise that Japanese mythology, along with Hawaiian spirits, have become an integral part of the multicultural spiritual vision of Island society.

The evidence thus far remains scanty and highly speculative. But the search leads to a drive-in theatre in Kaimuki, where in May 1959 strange sightings start in the ladies room of the Waialae Drive-In. Those reports supposedly continued for some two decades, until the drive-in was closed and the property developed for a housing project.

In this, one of the most famous of all local *obake* traditions, the haunting unfolds casually. Around midnight, a young woman goes into the restroom to freshen her lipstick. Standing at the mirror, combing her long, black hair is another young woman; the view of the face, however, is obscured by her beautiful, silken hair. As the first girl approaches the one at the mirror, she catches a reflection of the face—only, there is no face. Beneath the luxurious hair is a smooth, fleshy orb without evidence of mouth, eye, nose or ear. To add to the hysteria, the spirit at the mirror has no feet or lower limbs—the legs fade away into mist.

Several sightings of the faceless ghost of the Waialae Drive-In were followed by a newspaper article in which columnist Bob Krauss offered some explanations for the haunting. The drive-in, some said, was haunted by the spirits of a nearby cemetery that bordered the property. The manager claimed that the story was purely fictitious and, although some patrons complained that their friends had seen the phantom, none could produce a first-hand witness. Workers insisted that, even in the earliest hours of the morning, they had seen or heard nothing out of the ordinary. And yet the rumors persisted. Business for a brief time boomed as amateur ghost hunters crowded about the restroom waiting for a glimpse of the faceless woman ghost. Krauss intimated that children at Jarrett Intermediate School had but a week before reported seeing the same type of *obake*. The reasonable-minded amusedly suggested a clever hoax, while the curious repeated tales told by a "friend of a friend" that the lady of Waialae Drive-In was a genuine phantom.

In November 1982, during a local broadcast of a radio talk-show concerning Hawaii's ghosts, the old story of the haunted Waialae Drive-In surfaced. The station's switchboard immediately lit up—several listeners claimed to have personally seen the faceless lady ghost. One caller insisted that in 1980 she had gone into the restroom at the drive-in and had seen another girl combing her long, *red* hair in the mirror. She had evidently never heard about the resident ghost and therefore unhesitantly went up next to her to use the sink. Then she discovered that this red-headed girl had no face! Shrieking, she ran out of the restroom to get help. By the time she and her friends returned, the spirit had vanished. As long as the ladies room at that drive-in remained standing, unwitting females periodically reported having seen the faceless phantom.

What is unusual about this ghost story is the rarity of its type. The Waialae Drive-In seems to be the only place in Hawaii where a faceless spirit is seen. Even in Western, American and Polynesian ghostlore, faceless ghosts are rare or non-existent. A review of major folklore motifs reveals no international tales concerning monsters or ghosts without faces. Assuming for the moment that the faceless ghost of the Waialae Drive-In was a manifestation of generated folktale, where does it come from?

On a lonely portion of the Akasaka Road in Meiji Japan called "Kii-no-kuni-zaka," lonely travelers late at night would encounter a mournful woman, lying helpless beside the road. The night would be still and the moon would provide the only illumination. When a traveler passed by this sad female figure, he would hear crying. Asking what was wrong, he would be given no answer except more weeping. The kind traveler would insist that this was no place for a lovely young girl to be at midnight and that there was no need for tears. As he would implore her to leave that place in his safekeeping, she would slowly turn her face up towards the traveler, pulling back her hair. Horrified, he would discover that the weeping woman had no face. Wildly fleeing down the Akasaka Road, he would seek the assistance of an old peddler of buckwheat noodles, *soba*, who was also traveling the path. Upon hearing the traveler's unbelievable story, the *soba* seller would gently laugh as he raised a lantern to his own face. There, the hapless victim would see that the face of the old man also resembled that of the smooth surface of a white egg!

The faceless *obake* of Akasaka Road, as recorded by the romantic chronicler of Old Japan, Lafcadio Hearn, in his classic *Kawidan: Stories and Studies of Strange Things,* was called a Mujina. The Mujina was a faceless spirit that evidently haunted only the Kii-no-kuni-zaka portion of the Akasaka Road. While Hearn was far from being a scientific folklorist, many of the stories that he included in *Kwaidan* were collected from the villages of Meiji Japan—the Mujina was primarily a product of the folk imagination and not Hearn's fanciful literary mind.

That a Mujina should have appeared in Hawaii at the Waialae-Drive-In nearly fifty years after Hearn wrote down his tale is an exciting indication that Japanese *obake* do have the power to become multicultural Island phantoms. The Mujina in both the Hawaii and Japan tales are strikingly similar. Both seem to entice or attract their victims in solitary settings. There is something about the girl combing her hair in the restroom that compels the living to approach her—just as the crying girl on the Akasaka Road captured the sympathy of the passerby. Then, with a clever, frightening gesture, the Mujina slowly turn their heads so that the victim can only get a glimpse of the featureless face. The Mujina doesn't try to harm or attack its hapless subject—the sight alone of the hideous empty face is enough to incite panic and fear. In neither case does the ghost say anything, display mystical powers, or fly about the room. Its only purpose seems to be to frighten people with its "face."

The similarities are so marked to suggest that the origins of the Waialae Drive-In ghost might have very well been the Mujina of Hearn's tale. Whatever the visitors to the ladies room might have seen—a real manifestation of the supernatural, or a collective cultural nightmare compounded by the late hour, their isolation and fanciful imagination—the tale itself seems shaped in the retelling by a traditional Japanese motif.

What is significant is that the tellers of the story are frequently not Japanese—the drive-in has nothing to do with Japanese culture, no one has anything to do with Japanese culture, and no one has even suggested that the faceless lady was Asian—in one version she even has red hair! To the victims, the racial background of the faceless *obake* might really seem unimportant, but, to the collector of Hawaii's urban folklore, such a connection with ancient Japanese traditions illustrate the marvelous power ghost stories have in influencing what people believe and see.

The search for Japanese *obake* finding a home in Hawaii is even more interesting in the case of the Kappa. Almost every rural village in Meiji Japan had a tradition concerning these comic-looking creatures with deadly passions, who lived in rivers, ponds, lakes or the sea. The Kappa was an ugly, amphibious creature about the size of a small boy of three or four years of age. The creature's skin was a scaly greenish-yellow, its seaweed-like hair green and stringy. Its hands and feet were webbed, and on its back it wore a hard shell like a tortoise. The Kappa smelled like foul fish as it would sneak from its watery home in the dead of the night to steal vegetables from the villagers, disembowel horses and other livestock, rape women or drag young children into the pond, where it would pluck out their livers through their anuses. Not a very likable creature, the Kappa.

Parents would admonish their children to stay away from certain ponds in fear that the Kappa would drag them in to kill them. The devilish monster could disguise itself as a human child, and could then convince its unsuspecting victims to play push-pull finger near the edge of the water. When the fingers were hooked, then the Kappa would transform itself into its true being and yank the child into the pond. The only way to catch a Kappa was to empty the small saucer of water that rested on the monster's head. When it left the pond, the creature sustained its superhuman powers by the water carried in the built-in saucer. When the saucer emptied, the Kappa was helpless and an agreement could be made between the monster and the captor—in exchange for never harming another human being, the Kappa would be released. In this manner, certain villages and families had guaranteed themselves protection from the water monster.

For most second- or third-generation Japanese Americans in Hawaii, the Kappa, if they have ever heard of such a thing, is merely a fairy tale of Japanese lore read from a book or heard from the *issei*. Although no actual sightings of a Kappa have evidently occurred in Hawaii, the power of folk legends to generate themselves is strong.

The physical monster might not have immigrated with the *issei*, but its dangerous tricks, especially the inclination to drown children in ponds, continue to haunt certain Island communities. For example, in the late 1940s, in a village near Hilo, a story began concerning a small boy who had drowned in a pool of water. The body had been found sitting in a very natural position on a boulder at the bottom of the pond. The child's eyes were wide open; his position unnaturally reposed, as if he were sitting on a chair at home. Soon after his body was recovered and buried, other young children walking near the water would feel a force tugging on their pants or arms. It felt as if something were trying to pull them into the water. According to witnesses, another child was one day lifted up into the air by an invisible force and hurled into the pond, where he quickly sank. They recovered his still-living body sitting on a boulder in a manner not unlike the first victim.

The above story was collected from a *nisei* storyteller, who claimed that the tale was true—although the exact location of the pond, the main characters in the events, and other specific information were lacking. The "boy drowning in the pond" story seems to have its roots more in the popular Kappa folklore than in actual events.

However, a "true" ghost story of a "boy in the pond" did occur on Kauai in May 1951. According to newspaper accounts, Joseph Teves, 13 years old, and older brother Harold, 27, had drowned in January of that year in the Kapahi reservoir while fishing. In May, "Little Joe" began communicating with his 10-year-old sister. The sister would ask the spirit simple yes or no questions, to which Little Joe would respond by whistling once for "no" and twice for "yes." Scores of cars carrying neighbors, social workers, nurses, reporters and clergy crowded the Kapahi district, as over a hundred people crowded into the Teves home to hear the whistling boy of the pond. At one point, the cigar and cigarette smoke was so stifling the young girl fainted.

The family claimed they had first heard the whistling outside their house late at night. They thought originally the eerie sound might be the spirit of their grandfather, who they believed had come back from the grave. But, when the whistling began playing the tunes "Tennessee Waltz" and "Letter for Two"—Little Joe's favorites—they decided it must indeed be their drowned son.

The excited crowd in the Teves living room asked the spirit questions through the mediumship of the young girl. Was little Joe an angel? Yes, he was dressed in the garb of an angel and he was taller than when he was alive. A doctor who was present examined the girl and determined that she was not producing the whistles—her neck, mouth and throat didn't move when the sounds were heard. While she sat in on one part of the room, the whistles were distinctly heard coming from a far corner. Little Joe was even privy to special political knowledge—one witness asked him, "Did Truman do right by firing MacArthur?" The angelic answer was, "Yes."

As the excitement of the haunting continued, the whole island of Kauai seemed to arrive at the Teves doorstep. Police estimated that 2,000 cars were parked in Kapahi—those who couldn't jam into the house crowded about the windows and lawn. Some visitors asked the little girl to touch them in hopes of being cured of illness, although she claimed no such power.

On May 23, Honolulu radio station KTOH aired an interview or "seance" with the spirit of Little Joe. Listeners heard a voice whistle "The Bells of St. Mary's," "The Tennessee Waltz," and several cowboy songs. Little Joe implored listeners to go to church and pray for his brother Harold, who had also drowned. Then he informed the public that at five o'clock that evening he would return to heaven and never visit earth again.

Whatever the origins of the whistling, the excitement that the haunting of Little Joe caused was a fascinating glimpse into the supernatural interest and traditions of all Hawaii's people. That the boy should have drowned in a pond, and that his spirit could be heard calling from his watery grave, suggest that the Japanese tradition of demon ponds and drowned *obake* might have very well incited the community interest. Kauai has always had, afterall, a significant population of Japanese Americans. Little Joe was not a Kappa, nor was he killed by a water monster. But the "ghost of the pond," a widespread Kappa tradition, probably helped to lift this singular event into an island-wide attraction of curiosity, belief and supernatural faith.

Six years later, in April 1957, the Kappa legend surfaced again, causing hysteria and concerted community action. Half-a-dozen children attending Wahiawa Elementary school that year reported having seen what they called a "Green Lady" living in the Wahiawa Gulch behind the school gymnasium. Rumors of this strange creature rapidly spread among the children, leading the school's principal to suspect that "mass hysteria" was imminent. Police and reporters arrived at the scene and questioned the six children, all girls under 10, who described the Green Lady as having scaly, greenish skin and "seaweed hair." Her feet resembled those of a duck and her hands were claw-like. One of the girls said that the lady was also deformed—that she had no nose and only one ear. Another one thought it was simply someone in a Halloween costume, maybe a high school student playing a prank.

The Wahiawa Chamber of Commerce organized a search party that combed the gulch for the Green Lady, but found nothing. A police officer in charge of the investigation stated to the press that the whole incident was the result of a vivid imagination, "with subsequent elaboration by young and impressionistic minds."

But the Green Lady of Wahiawa was not confined to that area—children growing up near the present site of Makaha Elementary School in the early 1960s remember a similar Green Lady, who supposedly lived in the ponds and had "seaweed hair" and scaly skin. One informant revealed how as a child a Hawaiian man had told him to stay away from the swamp because "The

Green Lady will get you!"

The reality of the Green Lady need not concern us here. After living in Hawaii for several years, even the most die-hard skeptic refrains from hasty judgments concerning Hawaiian supernaturalism. However, assuming that the children had created the Green Lady out of their imaginations, it is curious how similar the Green Lady is to the Kappa. Either through oral transmission or simple fairy tales, the Japanese monster seems to have found a new home in the Hawaiian Islands.

Ghostly reports, such as the faceless ghost of the Waialae Drive-In, the drowned children of the ponds, and the Green Lady, will no doubt continue to exist as long as Hawaii's people continue to be fascinated by tales of the macabre and maintain their connections with their ethnic past. Perhaps the Japanese Kappa and Mujina have nothing to do with their Hawaiian counterparts—perhaps all of these ghostly sightings are completely independent of Japanese folklore. But, whatever their origins, our multiethnic community continues to be tantalized and excited by their continued presence. No matter how silly or absurd, the obake mirrors our hopes, our fears and puzzlement. And how barren and uninteresting a world it would be if Kappa and Mujina were not allowed to roam on still, dark Hawaiian nights.

Ghosts of a Plantation Camp: Thousands of Things Sinister and Dark

"There is something in this house that is trying to destroy us. It has already driven me to violence. I'm not sure I can keep my sanity."

The voice is sobbing and low. I ask her to wait one minute while I turn down the air conditioner in the office. It is almost impossible to hear callers on the telephone when the old clunker is rattling on. When I get back to the receiver, she seems under control.

"I'm not a psychic reader," I carefully explain to her. "And I don't bless houses or drive out devils. I'm not a priest or a specialist. All I do is collect ghost stories and I stay millions of miles away from haunted houses. So if you are . . ."

"I don't want your help, Mr. Grant. I just want someone who can tell me that I'm not crazy . . . that maybe other people see these things, too. My priest really doesn't believe me. And I know my mother thinks I've gone off the deep end. I was just hoping you'd say that other people have told you similar things."

People have told me thousands of things. Thousands of things that fill up cartons of cardboard file boxes, floppy data disks and scribbled memo pads. Thousands of things that have been dumped into my mental attic, where on quiet, lonely nights I find myself ascending to sort through cobwebs and nightmares. Other people's nightmares. Thousands of things, sinister and dark. Ghosts and spirits that pervade the substrata of this Island soil.

"Maybe you ought to start from the beginning so I can get a better idea of what kinds of things are happening in your house." Although it shouldn't be necessary, I must stress that the woman is not undereducated or illiterate. Some of you now sitting snugly on your little couch, secure in the protection of your home, perhaps suspect that those who experience the supernatural are superstitious or ignorant. However, over the course of many interviews I have discovered that the only difference between them and you is that, at this moment, you are safe. They are not.

In this case the caller is an intelligent Japanese-Hawaiian woman who works as a secretary in Haleiwa. She had never experienced anything paranormal until she and her husband moved into a small camp tucked back in the canefields surrounding Waialua. Her husband, a local Japanese guy, works for the sugar company and was provided free housing in the old camp. The settlement was once a thriving community, with churches, schools, temples, stores, a gymnasium and swimming pool. Once they were all young and ambitious, and their lives were filled with noisy activities and rich pleasures. Nothing of that remains now. The camp has an aura of decay, as if it were a corpse waiting only for final disposal. Only a few remaining homes now stand, housing the few workers who help support a dwindling industry.

The house the young couple currently occupy is one of these old plantation relics that has passed through several generations of workers. Although it is continually in need of repair, the house is compact, neat, and definitely not a dead end. They are ambitious. One day, she tells me in a moment of reflection, they had hoped to own their own home in one of the "bedroom communities" on the leeward side of Oahu. That dream seems farther away now that the unseen evil has begun to invade their lives.

It all began, simply enough, with the laundry. One afternoon, a few hours after she had hung her damp laundry on the clothesline, she discovered that it had disappeared. When she and her husband searched for the pilfered wash, they found it strewn about the roof of the house. Neighborhood children had obviously played a prank. The laundry was rewashed and rehung. Within the hour it had once again been thrown on the roof. When the couple confronted the neighborhood children with the "crime," they all, of course, denied having anything to do with it.

This would require, then, some ingenuity. The wash was hung on the line. She diligently watched from the kitchen window to catch the little pranksters. She waited . . . and waited. No children, no disappearing clothes. She remembers she looked away for only a minute. But that was enough time for the entire wash to be swept off the line and thrown in a heap on the roof. No one was seen entering or leaving the yard. That was the first moment that she remembers being truly frightened.

There would be other moments. And other things. Neighbors told her they saw the dark shadow of a man standing in the backyard of the house at night. A foul stench like decaying flesh was sometimes overpowering in certain rooms. And then there was that subtle, gnawing sensation that made you want to . . .

"Maybe you heard other stories that the camp is haunted?" she pleaded. "I mean, it's not all in my mind, is it? If it doesn't stop, then I'm afraid of what I might do!"

Rising from a fresh, green canefield in the Waialua district, there stands an ancient, withered cadaver, reaching out from the earth like so many arms reaching out of the grave. I must have passed Thomson's Corner a hundred times and never before noticed this shell of a burned-out old church, not 300 yards from the highway. It seems to me now that the "Obake Church" is the dominant landmark of mystery in Waialua, symbolizing the supernatural force that still pervades the plantation spirit.

Senior citizens from the Waialua Community Association had first given me an introduction to these ruins. As children of plantation workers, they had been told to stay away from the old church. Evidently, it was once a busy Catholic church that had burned down near the end of the last century. Rumors were rife that something special or mysterious lingered about the old sacred ground. One story circulated that the manager of the plantation, Mr. Thomson, had first wanted to tear the old walls down—but then he had a dream about the old church. In his dream, Mr. Thomson was instructed to leave the church alone—leave the walls standing. He was not a superstitious man. After all, wasn't he a *haole*? But he had enough respect in Hawaiian visions and beliefs to leave well enough alone. The walls, he ordered, were to be left untouched.

But still, it was an awfully dangerous place for children to be playing. So the parents, too busy working in the fields to supervise their children, used clever psychological devices that invariably produced the wrong results. If the pond and rivers were deadly, then tell the children that *kappa,* water monsters, would capture them if they went near those places. And if the crumbling walls of an old church were a potential death trap, then let it be known that it was an Obake Church filled with terrifying spirits.

Not a stone's throw away from the ruins, the kids found the infamous Hangman's Tree. Workers had once used the tree to hang Koreans, who in the once wild and lawless days of the plantation had committed terrible—but unnamed—crimes. The wind, when it blew across the canefields towards the ocean, would sometimes imitate the cries of a banshee . . . or maybe it was a Korean screaming in terror and pain.

Of course, none of these things could scare off the fearless, invincible Obake Club that was formed by the braver boys of Waialua back in the '20s. Once a year they defied their parents' warnings and ventured to the Obake Church in the dead of the night, lantern in hand, to see ghosts and terrible visions and to hear the screams of hanging Koreans. The first volunteer would walk alone into the ruins with the lantern, leave it within the walls and then return in the dark. The second boy would enter the church to retrieve the lantern and then, one-by-one, the process would be repeated in hopes that one of them would see the dreaded *obake.* Nothing ever happened.

Not that the church wasn't haunted. The story was told and retold by Japanese and Filipinos concerning the three young Portuguese fellows who had returned one afternoon from pig hunting in the hills beyond Waialua. They had captured and killed a wild pig, which weighed at least 150 pounds. They had wrapped it up in a gunny sack, tied the sack to a strong pole and begun the long trek home. Since the pig was heavy, they took turns hoisting the load over their shoulders. As time passed, they each noticed that the weight of the pig got a little lighter. They credited this to the fact that they were strong young men and they were probably just getting used to the load. However, by the time they passed the Obake Church, the weight of the pig was ridiculously light. They put the pole down and opened the gunny sack up to check on their meat. To their amazement and fright, the pig had utterly disappeared, leaving not a trace. The spirits of the Obake Church, they reasoned, had taken the pork as their own.

In the early plantation camps of Hawaii, these types of ghostly Hawaiian encounters were not unique experiences for Hawaiians, Japanese, Chinese, Filipinos, Puerto Ricans, Koreans or Portuguese. When the Japanese started arriving in the Islands in large numbers as contract laborers in 1885, those *issei* did not only bring their few personal belongings bundled in their wicker baskets and their avid desire for success—they also brought their ghosts that commingled and "intermarried" with indigenous Hawaiian spirits and those of other races. Every camp had its own hauntings, its *inu-gami* possessions, its *odaisans*, priests or priestesses who performed miracles and cures, its witchcraft and fear of *kahunaism*.

Since they lived in a foreign land with alien customs and beliefs, it was often the case that the immigrants had to "test out" the supernatural Hawaiian grounds. One *issei* recalled, for example, how he unintentionally urinated one day on the walls of an ancient *heiau*, or Hawaiian temple. Having just arrived in the Islands, he had no idea what a *heiau* was or how sacred they were to Hawaiians. That night he wet his bed. The next day he wet his pants while working in the fields. His control over his bladder eventually gave way totally and his clothing was in constant need of cleaning. The camp doctor had no explanation for his "sickness," but, while in a trance, an *odaisan* revealed to him the truth. She explained to him that he had desecrated a Hawaiian temple, and that until he washed the stones with Hawaiian salt and prayed for forgiveness, he'd never control himself. Taking her advice, he quickly learned the value of knowing something about Hawaiian culture and taught everyone he knew the care needed while urinating in Hawaii.

Other mysterious Hawaiian phenomena that the plantation workers encountered in Hawaii were what the Hawaiians call the *akualele* and Japanese call *hinotama*—fireballs. Believed to be the spirits of the dead returned, fireballs are glowing (often red) lights that can be seen especially in graveyards and lonely desolate roads. In Waialua, they have been seen along the old plantation railroads that once laced the countryside.

One evening, several of the men who worked on the trains had just returned to the rail yard. They were about to pack up and leave when they noticed a red, glowing light, perfectly round, at the end of the cars. Some of the men were holding lanterns, so at first they thought the strange light might be another man inspecting the back of the cars. They called out to him, but received no answer. One of them mounted his horse and rode back to the end of the cars to find the light's source. As he approached the red fireball, it backed away. Suddenly, the ears of his horse sprung forward and the animal, visibly frightened, stopped dead in his tracks. The light whipped around the back of the train, spun around overhead and then it got smaller and smaller until it disappeared. If the horse hadn't seen it also, the man would have believed he was hallucinating.

Before World War II, many of the residents of Waialua remember seeing what they called *"menehune lights"* stretching from Kaena Point and leading out into the sea. These "lights" appeared as fiery torches that seemed to be marching across the ocean horizon. One evening, a fisherman and his nephew were returning from a long day at sea, when the lights of the *menehune* appeared behind them on the horizon. The uncle had been drinking *okolehao* on the voyage home. Upon seeing the glowing lights, and feeling particularly brave in his drunken state, he swung his sampan around and began to chase them. The further out the sampan pursued the hovering, fiery torches, the further out the lights appeared. Every time it seemed that they had finally come within reach of the *menehune,* the lights suddenly seemed miles away.

Angry, the persistent uncle followed the evading spirits until much later he realized that they had been led so far offshore that they could no longer see the lights of Oahu. The sky appeared empty overhead; the stars dissolved into the inky blackness that was the ocean below and the heavens above. The only illumination was the yellow, flickering flame of their lantern and the distant torches of the spirit people luring them further and further into the other world. Praying for their souls, the uncle and boy stopped their mad pursuit and let the current return them to the lights and land of the living.

In another remarkable incident, the dark spirit of a man carrying a child had been seen standing in a plantation home, a vision which later resulted in the illness of one family member. When the dark spirit was finally driven out of the house, a bed rose up from the floor, turned on its axis, and threw its occupant out!

Of course, none of these experiences could directly help the young couple whose home was not under some sort of siege by sinister forces. As far as I had heard, the camp never had a spirit that hurled laundry about the yards. Yet who can predict the presence of ghosts who enjoy clinging to their earthly habitats? How many other families had once lived in their little plantation house? Perhaps 50 years ago another young couple had begun their life together only to find the all-too-familiar pain of jealousy, unhappiness, disappointment or violence. How much anguish, pain or remorse had someone once suffered in those rooms? Is the human experience so transient that none of the earlier emotional drama still lingers even when the flesh has long decayed and vanished? Do not some former shadows of unhappiness and sorrow remain?

"The worst thing took place this week, Mr. Grant. I was home with my little child, when I had an overwhelming desire to harm her. I was bathing her in the tub and, for some inexplicable reason, I started to hold her head under the water. She was struggling for air and I felt no sympathy, no guilt, no hatred. I was just like some kind of zombie killing my baby and feeling nothing. The water was splashing and she was kicking when my son came into the bathroom and asked, 'Mommy, what are you doing?' It was just like someone asking what you're cooking for dinner or something equally silly, and I suddenly saw my hands around my baby's neck, holding her down. What am I becoming? What's happening?" she implored.

"I'm letting my mother watch the children until this whole thing is straightened out. I'm not going back to that house. My husband isn't convinced yet, but I am. I know it's something in that house, something old and evil that wants us to hurt each other. It doesn't want us there. I know it sounds insane, but I'm not going back."

I could offer her no advice. Sharing her fears, absorbing her nightmares, I remember her trembling. Damn, the air conditioner must be on too high, I rationalized. Before she hung up the phone, she promised that she would keep me informed. That was almost three months ago, and I can only hope that her family and children are safe and warm and happy, just as you are. I want to believe that that plantation house, wherever its exact location, is empty and the haunted memories that desire to do harm have been vanquished.

Sunset at the cemetery located next to the Obake Church. The plantation has recently been burning cane and the fire must have gotten out of control, sweeping into the graveyard. Many of the headstones and graves, most of them containing Japanese immigrants, have been burned. The wooden markers are now nothing but scattered ashes. The stone and rock markers, with their chiseled Buddhist names having been blackened out, remain standing. My feet crunch the burnt brush and cane. Watching over one grave I discover an odd blue teddy bear. Rain and sun have weathered the little stuffed bear, who wears a faded red *palaka* scarf around its neck. Miraculously, the fire has not damaged the carefully placed toy. Teddy has his stubby little arms stretched out and is pleasantly smiling. He sits on a 30-year-old grave in which is buried three infant children. My skin begins to tingle as if a thousand bugs are crawling up my flesh. How pitiful is death and how lonely the vast puzzlement beyond.

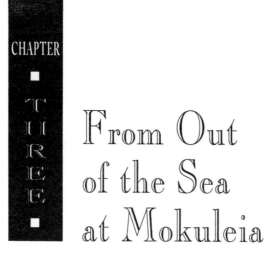

CHAPTER THREE

From Out of the Sea at Mokuleia

"Damn that Hiura, damn him."

I snuggled under my "waterproof" tarp that wasn't so waterproof anymore and fortified myself against the cool rain that fell heavy on the deserted beach. A cold wind whipped the raindrops like stinging missiles into my face and assaulted the expensive camera and tape recording equipment that I had wrapped in plastic shopping bags I had brought for this very purpose. Thank God, Star Market still gives a choice between paper and plastic.

My "scientific equipment" had been borrowed from The Hawaii Herald, and I knew (editor) Arnold Hiura would be really pissed at me if I damaged them in any way. The rain fell harder and, with a sputter, my little campfire went out. I turned up the propane on my lantern, clung to the tarp, and practiced every swear word I knew against the man (who I figured was probably sitting comfortably at home) for having talked me into this cockeyed assignment.

"You really blew it, Glen." We were sitting in Anyplace Lounge, our favorite local watering hole, about two months earlier. Arnold was carefully pointing out deficiencies in my personality as he ordered us a couple of beers. He was doing an excellent job of enumerating all of my recent failings, most notably the fact that I had missed contributing what had become my annual ghost story for the mid-October issue of the Herald last year. It was nice somebody cared.

"But geez, Arnold, I'm burned out. I mean, I don't think I can come up with something new to scare your readers. That *inu-gami* article was my triumph. It's been downhill ever since."

"Listen, man. We get requests every year for an *obake* article from you. You let us down last October. Don't let it happen again."

"I was going to do the story, but I went to Europe. I mean, I didn't have the time or . . ."

"Don't want to hear your excuses, Glen. You promised me something before you left. Then, next thing I heard you're traipsing who knows where. No telephone call, not even a postcard . . ."

Don't get me wrong. Arnold Hiura is a good person. And he is one of my best friends. But when he gets going, he'll twist your arm, foot, or any other part of your anatomy to get what he needs for his paper. I tried to beg off. I don't want to scare people anymore. I give up. . . I used every excuse I could muster. "Hell," I finally told him, "I've never even seen a ghost." To no avail.

His eyes suddenly gleamed with what I have learned to recognize as "editor's inspiration." "Why don't you set up a real ghost hunt? You know, spend the night alone at some haunted place. Take a camera and tape recorder and report what happens—a true, first-person account. Come on, it'll make a great story."

"You think I'm crazy? I don't fool around with this kind of stuff. I collect stories; I don't bother spirits. You've got to be an idiot to think I'd spend a night alone with the walking dead."

Two months later, I was shivering, alone, on Mokuleia Beach in a heavy rainstorm, cursing the name of one of my best friends. I was also trying to convince myself that the most active of spirits wouldn't come out on such a turbulent night.

By midnight, the rain had subsided long enough that I thought I could get the campfire going again if I could find some dry wood in the tangle of *haole koa* on the *mauka* side of the highway. If Arnold had at least let me drive my own car, I muttered to myself, then I wouldn't be soaking wet. Imagine—thinking I might duck out of my promise if I had my car! That (blankety-blank) promised he would pick me up at sunrise and he had better not be late!

I gathered what dry sticks I could and restarted the fire. By

24

then the sky had cleared and a billion stars illuminated the Hawaiian sky. I settled back with the surf gloriously before me on what had suddenly turned into an almost pleasant night. Thoughts of strange beings and supernatural phenomena faded almost completely as I checked the camera, waiting for what I knew was either a fanciful myth or one more inexplicable horror that lurked behind our reality. I practiced looking out of the eyes at the back of my head.

Fifty-five years ago, Mrs. Fumiko Kaneshiro and Katsumi Ebisu faced the horror from out of the sea at this very spot here at Mokuleia. According to Mrs. Kaneshiro, she was a young bride in those days, married to a "cowboy" on the Dillingham Ranch. Terae Kaneshiro had immigrated to Hawaii as an ambitious young man, had worked briefly on the sugar plantation, and, through a stroke of good fortune, had been hired as a cowhand on the small range started by B.F. Dillingham in the early years of this century.

There weren't many Japanese *paniolo* in those days, but Terae soon learned to excel at roping, branding and punching cattle. He bought himself a "10-gallon hat," leather chaps, cowboy boots, and a Mexican saddle with sterling silver trim. His photographs reveal a proud man on horseback, a brace of revolvers on his hips, staring resolutely into the camera, befitting the best Montana cowboy. Within a short time, he sent word back to his family in Fukuoka-ken that he was prepared to take care of a wife, and proper arrangements were made for Fumiko, a close friend of the family, to become his bride.

Over 70 years later, I met Mrs. Kaneshiro, now stooped and frail of health, through her daughter, a participant in the senior citizen program where I worked. "My mother has a ghost story to tell you," the daughter announced one day, and the next thing

I knew, I was sitting in their modest Kaimuki home, tape recorder in hand. The daughter acted as translator, for Mrs. Kaneshiro didn't want me to hear her pidgin English—even though I tried to assure her that I could probably understand her. Telling me of her experiences at Mokuleia in Japanese perhaps protected her from any doubts or skepticism she may have suspected from me. This is her true story.

"My husband and his friends often liked to go fishing," she explained through her daughter. "I was very lonely and frightened when I first came to Hawaii, so, when he and his friends went fishing, my husband was very kind to always take me along. While the men went fishing with their poles and nets along the shore, I would start a fire and cook food for them to go along with the *sake* they later drank. We always set up a tent on the beach and started a big fire.

"There were many places my husband liked to fish. When he could get a car, we would go to Mokapu. Kaneohe was a good place, and my husband liked it very much. And sometimes we would take horses and ride to Mokuleia, not far from Mr. Dillingham's ranch. That was very close, and we would spend the night sleeping on the beach.

"This one night, we rode down to Mokuleia and set up our camp. My husband and his friends went fishing as usual. They left me by myself, but I was not frightened, because then I did not know anything. I was very stupid about *obake* and things like that.

"So I was cooking dinner, when some other fishermen or campers moved in behind us. I never saw them drive up or ride their horses, but I knew they were there because they were talking story and laughing. There were many of them behind me, far away, maybe 100 feet or so. I looked hard in their direction, but it was very dark that night. There wasn't much of a moon, but I could see their lanterns. They were burning real soft, yellow. I never saw any people, but I heard them and saw their lights. They were talking in Hawaiian, or maybe English. I couldn't understand anything they said.

"My husband and the other men had been gone about an hour. They had gone far away from our campsite. But then, I noticed one of them coming up from the beach, walking towards me. I thought it was one of the men, and he must have taken off his shirt, because I could see his dark skin. His shoulders were very strong, and draped over them was a net he had dragged from the water.

"'Are you done fishing already?' I called out to him. He kept walking towards me but didn't say anything. 'Are you hungry?'

"Then I saw it wasn't one of my husband's friends. It was a Hawaiian man, wearing very little except some cloth around his middle. He kept coming towards me, but I couldn't see his face too well. Then the clouds passed from the moon for just a bit and I could see his face. He was maybe 40 years old, and he was staring at me like he was very angry with me. I still wasn't too scared, though, because the Hawaiian people had always been so nice to me.

"'Aroha,' I said with a smile. But he never said anything, still giving me a dirty look. 'Herro . . . ' I tried to say in English. But he still gave me the 'stink eye.'

"I had never seen a Hawaiian so mean before, and so I got scared. I wanted to offer him food, but I could see he wanted me to leave the place. This man did not want me here. I tried to say 'Aroha' again, when I noticed that something was funny about the way he walked. He moved very smoothly, like he was a bird sailing through the air. As he came even closer toward me, staring at me like I was something funny to look at, I finally saw why he walked so strange. He had no feet! From the knees down he had no feet, and he was floating towards me!"

At this point, Mrs. Kaneshiro started to laugh nervously and looked at me to see if I believed her. I had heard of many instances of floating apparitions without feet, I assured her, and asked her to continue.

"The Hawaiian man continued to scowl at me, then he moved off towards the other people who were camping behind us. As he left, I couldn't even scream or anything, but just watched with my mouth open. I wanted to tell those other campers to watch out. I wanted to help them. But as he walked towards them, their lanterns went out and they stopped laughing. I couldn't see the Hawaiian man anymore, and I realized I was alone, so I started screaming: 'Obake! Obake! Obake!'

"Some of the men came running back, my husband with them. He rushed up to me and asked me what I was talking about. I told him about the man looking mean at me, and his floating legs, and how the lights had disappeared when he walked toward those other campers.

"'What other campers?' my husband asked. I told him where they were, but by then the lights and sounds had gone away. He looked at me and I could see he didn't believe me.

"'Really,' I said. 'A ghost with no legs walked over there.'

"'Busheeto, *obake*,' he answered."

Mrs. Kaneshiro's daughter laughed when her mother told me of her husband's response. I assured her that I did not need a translator for this part of the story.

"'No busheeto. *Obake* are over there,' I answered, pointing to where they had been.

"My husband took a lantern and walked over toward the place where I had seen the lights. He was gone only a few minutes when he came running back, white as a sheet.

"'Pack up your things. Put out the fire. You guys saddle the horses. Come on, we're getting out of here!'

"'What's wrong? What's wrong?' I demanded.

"'That place, over there. It's a graveyard. An old Hawaiian graveyard.'

"In a few minutes I was ready to go. That beach was a scary place with or without *obake*. I wanted to get out of there. We were all packed and ready to leave when we realized that one of the men, Katsumi Ebisu, was missing. He had not come back with the other men, but must have been fishing way up the beach. I wanted to go home, but the men took lanterns and went calling for him. They were gone nearly half an hour when they came hurrying back carrying Katsumi. They laid him down on the beach and my husband asked me to look at him to see if I knew what was wrong. They held the lantern up over his face, and I felt a shiver go through my body. I had never seen anything so strange in my life.

"They had found Katsumi passed out on the beach. His shirt was ripped open—all the buttons torn off and the material shred-ded. His face and chest were all sweaty, like he had fever. But the spookiest thing was the color of his skin; the color of his skin wasn't normal—I'll never forget it. It was green—green like the color of grass. And he wouldn't wake up.

"I couldn't do anything, so my husband put Katsumi across the saddle of one of the horses, tied him on, and took him to Waialua for help. The rest of us went straight home, where I waited for my husband. He came home very early in the morning, before the sun came up. The doctor in Waialua was taking care of Katsumi, but so far they didn't know what was wrong with him. That night I asked my husband to hold me very tight while we slept. I thought I heard those spirits laughing, laughing all night long in that lonely land of Mokuleia.

"Two days later, we went to visit Katsumi. He was better and sitting up in bed. His wife was very scared that some demons had attacked him. We asked him what had happened, but he couldn't remember everything.

"When he heard me yelling '*Obake!*' he got scared, so he started pulling in his fishing net. That's when he knew he had caught something big. As he pulled it out of the water, he saw that it wasn't a fish in his net. It was a young Hawaiian girl. She was very beautiful. She laughed as she stood up and walked out of the water toward Katsumi. He backed away from her because she was acting *kitchigai,* and he thought she would hurt him. Suddenly, she darted forward, grabbed him behind the neck, and jumped on his back.

"Katsumi cannot speak English or Hawaiian, and so he's trying to find out what she wants. She wants a horseback ride, like a child, and she's whipping him like a horse. When he tried to throw her off, she got real mean. She tightened her grip around his neck and he felt her hot breath in his ear, and she licked him on the neck with her tongue. He was so scared, he did what she wanted, running around in little circles for her. With the flat of her hand she started slapping his okole and screaming and pulling on him to run faster and faster. He ran way up the beach for a few minutes. She was laughing and hitting him when he finally fell down.

"Getting off of Katsumi, the woman then rolled him over and sat on his chest. She ripped off his shirt, the buttons flying in the air. He struggled to get up, but the force of her hands and arms were so great that he couldn't move. He tried to scream, but only a gurgle came out. The moon was coming in and out behind the clouds, casting wild shadows on the woman's face; the sound of the sea was roaring not 10 yards away. Then this Hawaiian maiden opened her mouth, slipping her tongue between her moist, dripping lips."

Mrs. Kaneshiro said that Katsumi was shivering in his bed as he related what happened next. She told her husband later that she couldn't believe what Katsumi said next, but the memory of the horrible green skin kept coming back to her.

As I sat on the desolate beach at Mokuleia, I kept imagining episodes in Mrs. Kaneshiro's story and the disgusting things that happened to Katsumi Ebisu during his tryst with the creature disguised as a woman. I could see her propped up over him, her tongue emerging from her mouth—sharp, darting and dripping with saliva. It coiled in her throat like a slimy eel and slowly emerged to strike at his face. Out her tongue came, until the moist, bright red muscle was no less than three feet long. She started with his face, licking all the salt and sweat from Katsumi's face as he lay terrified, unable to move or scream.

Eagerly she licked his perspiration, lapping across his cheeks and forehead, chin and eyes. Down to his chest and neck went her long, hideous tongue. As she held her head back, recoiling her sated tongue, she let out a cruel, triumphant laugh, as Katsumi lapsed from consciousness and fell into a two-day, nightmare sleep. What scared me the most about Mrs. Kaneshiro's story, in addition to its authenticity and the conviction on the part of its teller, was the uncanny similarity between her tale and far more ancient stories concerning Mokuleia. After my meeting with her, I went to "Sites of Oahu," a Bishop Museum publication cataloguing many of the legends and history of the island. In the Mokuleia district, according to old accounts, was a *mo'o*, or water creature (often thought to resemble a lizard), that could disguise itself as a beautiful woman. Another of its powers was its ability to disguise its large tongue as a surfboard.

That immigrants from Japan to Hawaii would have concocted such a tale, so peculiarly tied to ancient Hawaiian beliefs, struck me as improbable. I asked her daughter if Mrs. Kaneshiro was a student of Hawaiian folklore. She assured me that her mother had not read things about Hawaii. Whatever happened on the beach that night to terrify the fishermen was not from any book of folklore. It was real, and it was there.

"Damn, Arnold."

I must have reiterated that oath a hundred times. I hoped he was having as miserable a night as I was. I blamed him and myself for the ridiculous bargain we had struck. Who gives a damn about the Herald readers, I complained to myself. I'm sitting out here all night amidst threatening spirits just so they can have their scary story? I kept a sharp eye on the ocean before me, while the eyes on the back of my head were focused on the cemetery across the road. The night stretched on, the fire went out, and, sometime around 4:00 in the morning, I leaned back and fell into a well-deserved sleep.

When Arnold woke me up around 7:30 a.m., my face had been breakfast for little sand fleas, but I was alive, unattacked and "unghosted." He had the nerve to scold me for the sand in his camera, but I told him it was a small price to pay for the long, boring night I had spent on the beach at Mokuleia.

Then, about a month ago, as I was preparing this article on the "uneventful ghost hunt," I reviewed my notes and evidence taken that night on the beach. My photographs were very poor; the ASA had not been set correctly, so most of the pictures revealed nothing more than the yellow flame of my campfire.

Then I played the tape back so I could listen to all of the expletives I had hurled at Arnold that night. I was using my cheap, old tape recorder at home, wading through the "damns" and other comments, when my girlfriend asked me what that sound was in the background. The surf or some night insects, I assured her.

"No, not that sound. Listen, it's like a tiny whine." Patronizing the dear woman whose imagination is far more flexible than my own, I replayed and replayed it for her. I still could not determine anything—at best, there was a frail, tinny sound—very high-pitched. She insisted I play the tape back on better equipment.

I called my friends at the Media Center at the college where I used to work and asked them if I could use their sophisticated recording equipment. The next day, arrangements were made for me to use a small studio, where I could hear portions of the tape magnified and clarified to a degree beyond the capabilities of the human ear. I asked the technician if there had been a mistake, or if the tapes had somehow been replaced. No, he assured me, it was the tape I had brought in.

He asked me where the tape had been recorded and why I was turning so pale. I explained that the tape was made that night on the beach at Mokuleia, in the morning, just before I had given up and gone to sleep. I had been, I thought, perfectly alone. I had seen, felt or experienced nothing. And yet, there on the tape was what seemed to be a human voice, calling, as if across an inky void. Tears welled up in my eyes as the technician and I exchanged looks of disbelief. For there on the tape, barely discernible, was the sound of laughter . . . and a few simple words.

"You're next," I heard it whisper in horror. "You're next."

Dear reader, it will take much more than my feeling of goodwill towards you and my friend Arnold Hiura to pursue his plans for next year. I will not, I repeat, will *not* spend a night alone in a haunted hotel room. After this year's strange events, I have concluded that I, Glen Grant, do not exist to serve as a guinea pig for other people's curiosity about the supernatural. I suggest you contact someone else, anyone else. As for me, I do not plan on venturing over to north side of Oahu for many, many years.

Inugami: An Investigation Into A Case Of Dog Spirit Possession

I've been warned many times by my friends that the strange, uncanny stories I sometimes pursued would one day do me harm. While I have hitherto ignored such advice, back in October 1984 I found myself falling irretrievably into the bizarre, mythic world of my own stories.

The following story is related in a series of rambling, disjointed notes, for, as my actual notes of that experience reveal, it was impossible for me to devote myself to writing a well-organized, scholarly piece. Extraordinary events consumed my time and mind with a halcyon of impressions, fears and dreams.

Because the events described in my journal seem unbelievable, I have augmented my notes with corroborative testimony from a fellow researcher, Ray Funamoto, who was working with me at the time. Even today, I shiver in fear as I look back on the events as they unfold in the following entries.

(From My Research Journal)
July 22. Moiliili. At 1:30 p.m. this afternoon I am contacted by supernatural researcher Ray Funamoto that a "friend" has seen our television interview on KHON-TV and would like to share information he has about a "haunted" house located next to his

in Nuuanu Valley. I explain to the "friend" that I merely collect stories and am not a trained investigator of the paranormal. He retorts that priests, *kahuna, odaisan,* even a Portuguese *fatsetta,* or witch, have been brought into the house and have all verified the hauntings. If I want a real story then the family is willing to share their experiences with us. He refuses to specify the nature of the haunting. Arrangements are made to visit the house early the following week.

July 25. Puunui. Ray and I arrive at the Puunui home of our informant at 7:30 p.m. He greets us with beers on his front lanai overlooking a quiet residential street and begins by explaining that he has known his victimized neighbors for about six years. They are a quiet nisei couple in their early fifties with good government jobs who have one child—a 22-year-old daughter named Dawn who recently graduated from the University of Hawaii. For the past two months, Dawn has not left her home. Right after her graduation in May, she suddenly quit her job at a department store and concealed herself in her bedroom. One evening about two weeks ago our informant states that he and his wife heard horrendous screams coming from one of the back bedrooms—it sounded as if Dawn and her parents were trying to kill each other. He called the police, who soon arrived and then left, apparently reassured by the parents that all was in order.

Early the next morning Dawn's father, obviously ashamed and contrite and looking as if he hadn't slept for several days, appeared at the neighbor's door. He apologized for all the disturbance the previous night and then broke down, claiming that he and his wife were at their wit's end. Dawn, he said, had retreated into what could only be described as an extreme psychotic state. She wouldn't eat; she never left her room; her language was foul and abusive; her hygiene habits, usually impeccable, had become in the politest term, disgusting. She was no longer their daughter. At first they thought that her condition was an outgrowth of her breaking up with her long-time boyfriend. But as the condition worsened, they realized that it was something far more tragic. She hadn't gone to see doctor, nor could they entice her to do so. When the family doctor visited, she barricaded herself in her room and called him obscene names. They were terribly ashamed. They had even tried calling in a famous Nuuanu Valley *odaisan*, a kahuna, a Catholic priest and a *fatsetta*, all to no avail. They prayed at their *butsudan* constantly for the peace of their daughter's soul.

As I listen to this story, I think how often psychological disturbances of this kind are called "hauntings" by ill-informed people who have no grasp on reality. From the lanai I quietly watch the Pali saddleback so beautifully visible from Puunui and nurse my beer. I glance next door at what seems to be a perfectly normal middle-class Hawaii home. There is only a soft, yellowish light illuminating the front parlor in an otherwise blackened house.

"So what makes this house so 'haunted.' I mean, I haven't heard anything that would . . ." He interrupts me with a long, low laugh.

"There's something going on in that house," he assures me. He asks if we are ready to go over and visit with Dawn's family. As we walk the short distance across their yard, I ask him why the family has agreed to allow Ray and myself to enter the house. Surely, this is a private family matter for doctors or religious people. As we got to the front steps, he briefly answers that Dawn had once been one of my students at the University and she asked for my presence. I feel a deep discomfort in my stomach.

From within the house comes a loud crash of dishes and a familiar four-letter expletive. Ghost researcher or not, this doesn't seem to be any of my business. "What does the *odaisan* say is the matter?" He hesitates, then softly answers, *"Inu-gami."*

Ray and I exchange glances. I make a flimsy excuse that we are not yet ready for this encounter, and, promising to call, we beat a hasty retreat to Moiliili.

July 26. Moiliili. I suspect something is amiss, a suspicion confirmed when I can find no trace of "Dawn" in my class records or memory. Ray and I postpone our next appointment at the haunting. We begin a survey of the literature on Japanese *inu-gami*, or dog spirit possession, which is said to destroy the body and soul of hapless human victims.

August 15. Hamilton Library, University of Hawaii. Three weeks of research in the library supplies a much-needed overview of *inu-gami* in Hawaii:

Background

Inu-gami witchcraft folklore among Hawaii's Japanese Americans is an outgrowth of older Shinto beliefs that issei immigrants transported from Japan. Polytheistic and animistic in structure, Shintoism encompassed older beliefs of the indigenous population of Japan before the introduction of Buddhism from China. Essential to Shintoism is the concept of omnipresent *kami*, or gods. Every animate and inanimate creation is imbued with the spirit of *kami* so that Japanese folk religion is pervaded with spirits guarding every room in the house, the most minor of household objects, fields, crops, seasons—the whole substance and cycle of rural agriculture life. The *kami* can also appear as demons, evil spirits employed through magic and witchcraft to harm human beings. The demons of animals which cause illness, insanity and demonic behavior in their victims are especially feared.

One of the most dreaded forms of Japanese folk witchcraft in Hawaii has been the *inu-gami*. John Embree in his monograph on Japanese in Kona during the 1930s recorded several instances of the practice, most notably *inu-gami* possession, in that Big Island region. Sen. Spark Matsunaga, whose father was an *ikibotoke*, or living saint who exorcised animal possession, remembers that *inu-gami* was "very prevalent" in the late-1930s on Kauai. Student informants at the University of Hawaii report similar outbreaks of *inu-gami* in the 1940 plantation camp of Kalaoa, near Hilo, and during religious exercises conducted among the Japanese of Honolulu in 1941. Although not common, *inu-gami* possession still occurs in modern day Hawaii.

Inu-gami Witchcraft

In traditional folk practice, animal possession was a result of witchcraft directed against one's enemy by a witch who had been able to capture the spirit of an animal. The type of animal used for these evil purposes—fox, badger, cat, snake, monkey or dog—varied from region to region in Japan, each prefecture preferring its own animal. That the *inu-gami* is prevalent in Hawaii is simply explained by the fact that most immigrants to Hawaii came from the Inland Sea regions of Japan (encompassing Shikoku, parts of Kyushu, Awa, Hiroshima and Yamaguchi prefectures), areas rife with dog spirit belief. Within each Japanese village there were those "witches" who were recognized to be in possession of the *inu-gami*. These *inu-gami- moichi* were said to have captured the spirit of a dog which they could send out to do harm against their neighbors or rivals. The method of capturing the dog spirit was simple enough: a dog is tied up and systematically driven mad through slow starvation.

When the dog has become nearly rabid, its body is buried in the ground, leaving the head fully exposed. The witch then puts a large piece of fresh raw meat in front of the dog, but out of its reach. As the dog savagely struggles to eat the meat, its head is cut off and concealed in a special *inu-gami* shrine. Fervent praying by the witch and offerings of rice and beans evoke the spirit of the dog which, for the price of food, will do the bidding of the witch. Hungry and enraged, the evil animal spirit will invade the body of those who are the envious or vengeful enemies of the witch.

The victims of this *inu-gami* witchcraft undergo varying degrees of demonic possession. *Inu no tatari,* or dog curse, is in most cases a form of possession where the victim will first become physically ill, mentally unbalanced, or criminal in behavior. Recognizing or suspecting symptoms of *inu no tatari,* a Shinto priest or healer is brought to the victim for exorcism rites. In the presence of the healer who prays over the victim—sometimes striking them with a pompom-like wand to drive the dog out—

the possessed will begin to act like a dog, running about on hands and knees, barking, writhing on the floor, and even foaming at the mouth. Usually, the healer speaks to the animal spirit who can be bribed with food to leave the possessed alone.

August 16. Moiliili. Is our strange case of "Dawn" a modern-day reoccurrence of *inu no tatari*? Psychological symptoms seem the overriding concern far outweighing supernatural theories. Her separation from her boyfriend seems the triggering event, as well as perhaps her graduation into adulthood. Parents have become desperate and have requested our presence at an exorcism to be performed this week.

August 18. Puunui. The events of this evening still twirl my mind. At 8 p.m. Ray and I are ushered into a small parlor by Dawn's parents. As we meet the parents for the first time, I note how extraordinarily average they and their home seem. I am struck by a series of framed photographs that are on one of the built-in bookcases it is the progression of their daughter from infant to child, to adolescent and young adult. She is certainly attractive. The most recent color photograph shows her in her University of Hawaii cap and gown. The frame is bedecked with colorful yarn leis and a maile wreath that still appears fresh. You can sense that her parents adore her.

"Have there been any manifestations accompanying your daughter's illness?" Ray's question draws a puzzled look from the parents. "You know, flying objects, cold spots, *obake* shadows, that kind of thing."

"Mr. Funamoto," the father curtly replies, "I haven't seen any-thing. I don't care about those kinds of things. We only care about our daughter. Can you understand that?" He is trembling, and we are intimidated by the reality, and sincerity, of what we have stumbled into.

"Mr. Grant, Dawn seems to have real confidence in you. She's asked for you and seems to think, maybe . . ." I really can't re-member ever knowing her. "Why don't I go in and see her," I volunteered, not meaning a single word of it.

She is in her bedroom guarded by an elderly Japanese woman

who is the *odaisan*. Dawn is sitting with her back to the door in a high-back rocking chair. She is evidently wrapped in a blanket. Her father and I enter the dimly lit room alone, circling around to the front of the chair. I keep picturing the photograph of the attractive young U.H. graduate on the bookshelf, expecting to see her as I gently call out, "Dawn," as if waking someone from a sound sleep. Her head is down, her face covered with matted, unwashed hair caked with her own filth. Then I hear a clammy, fetid voice emit a sound like, "Glen?"

"Yes?"

"I knew you'd come, you a—hole." It shoots out at me with a terrible vehemence as she flings her head back laughing gutturally. Her face is yellowish blotched, and the eyes are filled with lean hunger and vengeance. The rocking chair begins to rock madly on its legs, as if it's driven around the room by a demonic engine. She continues cackling—my heart pounds as I'm frozen in place, the chair is still spinning about the floor. I swear that it sometimes lifts off the floor. The *odaisan* is flaying the pompom wand screaming *"Ka-e-re!"* ("Go home!"), as if driving out the evil spirit. The father reaches to shield his daughter from her own evil, and without rising from the chair, she lifts the man off the floor and flings him into one of the walls.

"I'll kill you if you touch me! I'll kill you!" At that moment a shrill and terrified scream from the front room broke the tension. Everything in the room broke the tension. Everything in the room, including Dawn, became still. I knew that banshee scream had come from my cohort Ray, and without delay, or excuse, I dash out of the bedroom. What happened to Ray must at this point be told in his own words...

(Funamoto's Notarized Testimony)

The following is a true statement. These are the facts, just as they happened on the night of August 18 in Puunui.

As Glen Grant went that night into the bedroom to talk with Dawn, I entered the kitchen to get a glass of water. The room was uncomfortably dark, and as I went to the refrigerator, I heard a faint sound which became louder. It was the distinct sound of an ukulele being played by a young Hawaiian girl with a rather pretty, smiling face and her shapely, bare breasts unabashedly exposed. She sang her melody and waved at me, seemingly beckoning from outside the window. At first I was entranced by the pleasant song and charms of the ghostly dancer until I noticed one feature about her that stirred a feeling of unease in me. Her eyeteeth displayed in the smile were quite long and pointed—like an animal's, while her eyes, though normal shaped, were dark and seemingly bottomless. At that point I did a stupid thing—I showed her fear by recoiling from the window. Seeing or sensing my fear, she moved closer, her hands passing through the window, followed by her body. I then screamed and fled the kitchen when the others in the house rushed to my assistance. I am certain the vision of that Hawaiian girl was real, and I believe she is a lost, unhappy spirit perhaps buried beneath the house.

(Research Journal)
September 3. Moiliili. It has been several weeks since the unsettling events recorded in my last entry. I have avoided making new arrangements to visit the house, despite the parents' insistence that since that terrible night Dawn seems remarkably improved. She has asked to see me so that she can apologize. I promise to visit as soon as possible.

I am still not convinced that we are dealing with genuine *inu-gami* possession. The girl neither acted nor sounded like a dog in my encounter. The episode with the rocking chair and the superhuman strength is certainly remarkable, but not wholly unexplained by natural causes. As to the bare-breasted hula girl seen by Ray—investigation under the house did not reveal any Hawaiian graves.

September 24. Puunui. Ray has just dropped me off at home after an hour and a half at St. Francis Hospital's emergency ward. It is nearly midnight and my face, neck, arms and shoulders are a painful, tender mess of stitched gashes and scratches.

I knew we should have left this "Dawn" case alone. I sensed it would lead to danger. The parents said it was a dinner to celebrate their daughter's complete recovery. They should have said temporary remission.

She was actually pretty at the dinner table—pretty to the point of flirtatious. Ray, enthralled by her girlish charm, doted over her. She ate a full meal and didn't seem too worse for wear from her *inu no tatari.* She told me how much she enjoyed my class when she was at the UH (she identified the class and semester, though I insist I have no recollection of her). Then about 8:30 she excused herself, saying she was tired and would like to rest in her room. She kissed her happy, beaming parents "Good night," thanked me and Ray once again for our trouble, and quietly retired.

Just as we were making our final rounds of "thank yous" and "delicious meal" and "no need to go" and "oh, but we must" with the parents, Dawn calmly called out from behind her closed door, "Papa, come!" She sounded little-girlish and her father, so thankful to have his daughter back, didn't heed the sign that instinctively told me "abandon hope all ye who enter." He crossed the room and silently shut the bedroom door behind him.

It wasn't a scream or any other classic horror story device that broke the evening. It was a low, rumbling earthquake that shook the walls and floor and toppled the pictures on the bookcase. It lasted only a few seconds, but it seemed catastrophic. I called out to Dawn's room if she and her father were alright. I received no answer, so I entered the pitch-dark room. Behind me I heard Ray and the mother picking up broken dishes and muttering oaths in Japanese. In the light of the open door I saw the father lying unconscious on the floor, at the foot of the bed.

Above me, on the bed, I heard the vicious growl of a dog. Right by my neck I felt its hot panting breath and wet saliva. It was crouching, waiting to pounce on me. I wanted to move, but I sensed with every movement the animal would bear down closer, its muscular jaws ready to rip into my throat. It had me trapped. I moved forward, inch by inch, breaking the spell it had over me until I could slowly turn my head to see the beast. Only it wasn't a dog. It was Dawn. But it was a dog.

The sheets were damp with her blood. Each nail had been ripped from the fingers and thumbs of both her hands. The bloody pulp was transforming itself into paws, and vicious claws were quickly growing. She bared her canine teeth, and, before I could escape, my face and neck and upper torso had been slashed and blood blurred my eyes and a savage dog snarled and ripped and I was hysterical and a frightened Ray rushed me down the street to St. Francis Hospital trying to explain to the interns how I had received my hundred wounds.

October 10. Kaunakakai Wharf, Molokai. The best cure is a retreat, and if I am to escape the evils of Honolulu, then Molokai seems distant and peaceful and absent from curses and *obake* and things I should have left alone. The doctors claimed that she really did lose her fingernails. She ripped every one out. Although they urged me that she didn't have paws or long canines. She did bark. All *inu-gami* victims bark.

I never noticed how many dogs there are in Hawaii. They are all over. Unleashed.

We checked, and there was a slight earthquake on Oahu the night of September 24—although seismologists claimed it could not have done the damage we described in Puunui.

I have no idea what has happened to Dawn. To be honest, I don't give a damn. I'm not talking to Ray. You see, he studies *obake* more than I do. He knows the Japanese language. He has good reason to be the *inu-gami-moichi* that caused all this. He's jealous of me. I know that. I'm convinced. He's sent it out for me, but Molokai is too far away.

I haven't gone to work in weeks. My face is still healing. I told everyone I broke up a fight between two bar girls. Very macho.

Molokai is so peaceful. I don't have those dreams. Yet. The *fatsetta* says she can rid me of my *inu-gami*. It makes you wonder, doesn't it? I mean, take a look at your dog. Can you trust it?

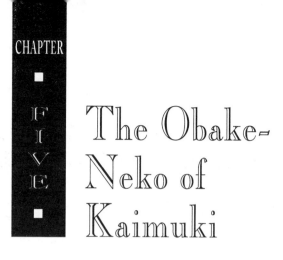

The Obake-Neko of Kaimuki

Prologue

After a story I had written entitled "Remarkable Case of Inu-gami Possession" was published in The Hawaii Herald, the reaction to that article was amazing. It ranged from those who offered to help exorcise the victim, to those who were concerned about my own physical and mental well-being. Most, however, simply wanted to know, "Was it true?"

One such person was Lance F., a graduate student at the University of Hawaii at Manoa. He contacted me not long after the article appeared, explaining that he had an interest in parapsychological phenomena and was conducting research into the history of demonic possession. He wanted to see me regarding additional information on Japanese styles of *inu-gami* belief in Hawaii.

I was at first very reluctant to discuss the matter, wanting to "lay low" for a while to let talk about the article pass. Lance was persistent, however, arguing that his research would perhaps complement my own. I finally told him that I wasn't researching the supernatural anymore, but, if he had an open mind, I would meet with him.

My desire to dissociate myself from the *inu-gami* case was real—I had never mentioned it again in the two years since the article had appeared. But what started out as an apparently innocent inquiry soon developed into one of the most bizarre cases I have ever encountered. The following research notes, excerpts from interviews, and Lance F.'s personal diary speak of many strange things going on in modern Hawaii.

As a scholar, I can testify that the physical phenomena as described are real. As an educated person, I want to believe that all the causes of the phenomena are natural and rational. As a human being, I am frightened. I choose to share this information now in the hopes that if any of you have the curiosity that compelled Lance F. to pursue his unusual interests, you will, as I have, abandon them immediately.

An Interview With Lance F.

On December 2, 1984, I finally arranged a meeting with Lance F. He had just returned from an extended visit to Kauai, where, he told me, he was having "a much-deserved escape from pressures in Honolulu." I agreed to meet him at his small studio apartment on 9th Avenue in Kaimuki.

When I arrived at his home, he greeted me into what was certainly one of the most unkempt, dingy apartments I have ever had the misfortune to enter. I kept my slippers on because I wasn't sure that the floor was wholly inanimate—my first impression was that small roaches formed a living carpet. The curtains were pulled tight, allowing no light, although it was mid-afternoon— the small kitchenette had dishes piled high with a thin growth of mold forming on the plates. There is no further point to describe the filth, except to say that the floor, bookshelves, bed and chairs were draped with tons of popular occult literature from Ouspensky and Ruth Montgomery to authors on Japanese ghostlore—a copy of my *inu-gami* article lay on the floor.

If anything was even more unkempt than the studio, it was Lance himself. His clothing was unwashed and disheveled. His hair was uncombed and had already outdistanced his ears. Upon his face were several deep gashes that resembled the marks of nails or claws. I noticed the same marks upon his arm, neck and chest. It looked like an animal had attempted to tear him apart. Most remarkable were the man's eyes. I can never forget that wild look—it was if he was another person trapped within an unwanted body.

Extracts of the interview I conducted that afternoon follow:

"In the *inu-gami* article you stated that all the stories were based on truth. Had you personally witnessed any cases of dog spirit possession?" Lance began.

"Everything I wrote in that article was based on two different cases I had heard about from priests who had exorcised the young girls who were purportedly possessed by the *inu-gami*. The essentials of the story were true, I just said I was there at the time of the possession," I explained.

"So it wasn't true that you had been personally attacked by one of the girls?"

"No. I used my imagination."

"Why?"

"Because I wanted to frighten the readers a little. That's why. Everyone likes to be frightened."

(At this point in the interview, Lance became very agitated. His voice became more tense, as if he would burst into tears at any moment. I had come to his home basically to discuss the nature of inu-gami possession, but he quickly began talking about his personal problems. He told me how he had lost his part-time job at the University, how his friends had deserted him, and something about a broken heart. I felt embarrassed and apprehensive about becoming the man's psychiatrist.)

"Do you believe that the cases of *inu-gami* you've investigated are caused by . . . well . . . ghosts or spirits?" Lance asked.

"Oh, yes, definitely."

"You see, everything was going quite well in my life until you wrote that damned article. I'd been reading ghost stories only as a 'hobby,' but suddenly this *inu-gami* thing got hold of me. Soon after the article came out, these stupid dreams started," he confided.

"What dreams?"

"I didn't tell you about the dreams? Why do you think all my friends left me? Cause of these stupid dreams I talk about all the time, I've driven everyone away, except maybe my mother . . . but hell, she lives on Maui and all she knows is that her crazy son wakes her up with long-distance calls telling her about his dreams."

"Can you tell me about them?"

"Yeah. I guess that's the *real* reason I called you to begin with. Less than two months ago, right after I read the article, I was sure I was . . . possessed by a dog. Don't laugh. I know it sounds ludicrous, but after that first dream it seemed that every damn animal in Honolulu was taking turns coming into my bedroom at night. My God, I know it sounds incredible, but these dreams have ruined my life. Here, take a look at some of my diary entries."

(At this point Lance showed me a small book which he called his "dream diary." These are a series of dreams he began to jot down in the middle of the night when he awoke from his nightmares so that later he could clearly remember them.)

October 24. 2:30 a.m. "I am lying in my bed with my back to the bedroom door. I remember leaving the front door open and becoming concerned that I should shut it. As I begin to move from the bed, I feel a presence in the bedroom, on my bed, immediately behind me. As I move, it becomes angry and desperate. Its hot breath is on my neck and I can almost feel the steamy saliva on my ear. It growls deep and viciously. Every move I try to make, it follows me until I realize that it wants me to submit myself to it. At that moment it begins to push its entire body into mine. I can't describe it except to say that I feel as if my soul is being displaced by this beast. While I am frightened, it feels strangely satisfying. I am accepting the new spirit when I wake up in a sweat."

Just reading a few of the entries gave me chickenskin—every dream was exactly the same. Nearly every night was noted, from October through November, as a night of what he called the "Inu-gami Dream." I asked him if he didn't think that it was his imagination.

"Yes," he said. "It was my imagination playing tricks on me. But how do you explain the scratches?"

"What do you mean?" I asked.

"When I wake up from the dream, the scratches are on my body."

I ended our first interview and promised to keep him informed of any research phenomena I uncover of similar scratch marks appearing on a possession victim. His earlier reticence was replaced with a sincere desire for a friend, a fellow replaced into all this spirit inquiry. I agreed to call him in a few days and gladly got out of his little studio apartment, promising myself that the next time I would meet him at the Kaimuki recreation center, or some other neutral ground.

I didn't call him back. He called me, inviting me back for more talk. The dreams had changed, he told me. At last the dogs had left him. I told him I was pleased and that maybe in a week or two I would meet him at Zippy's on Waialae and by then I would have some information. He declared he wouldn't read another book about ghosts, spirits or possession. I became, reluctantly, his personal researcher and counselor. I did feel sorry for him.

December 10: I have agreed to meet Lance again. I have resolved not to let this investigation of his dream evolve into more personal fantasies. The man has no evidence of any supernatural visitation except the facial and body scars that could be self-inflicted.

On December 15 I met Lance at the Zippy's restaurant on Waialae Avenue, as prearranged. His clothes looked a bit more orderly, although his hair was still unkempt, his teeth yellowed from neglect, and his eyes burning with that fury that made looking directly at him too distracting. The scars on his face had healed, but he was still obviously agitated. The following is a tape transcription of what he told me that day:

"Since I last talked to you, Dr. Grant, the dreams have totally gone away. And they haven't come back. Whatever was bothering me, is gone. Now that I think back, I guess reading that article and having personal problems wasn't a good combination. Yeah, now that I think about it, I probably was scratching myself in the night. Anyway, the reason I wanted to talk to you was that I am in love! I mean, really in love. This girl is incredible."

(I tried to get out of the interview at this point, but he kept right on going. I didn't want to get into his personal feelings, etc.)

"I met her at one of those bars down at the edge of Waikiki, you know the one near the Ilikai? I was in there having a drink, and she just sits down right next to me and smiles. I buy her a drink, and the next thing I know we're talking about Japanese movies and classes she's taking at the UH and where do I live—and how nice Kaimuki is and all that stuff. I mean, Dr. Grant, this is the most beautiful girl I have ever seen. I mean, for a local girl she's got a great body and aggressive and a real turn on."

"She sounds great," I answered. "Does she have a sister?"

"I don't know. In fact I don't know too much about her, except that we're together almost every night."

"I'd like to meet her," I said, not meaning a word of it. This guy was more than a little odd.

"I don't think you can, Dr. Grant. I mean, Dorie is a dream. She started coming after the dog left. But I mean this is better than real life. I swear it. I'd give up a month with Jessica Lange for one night with Dorie." He laughed a high, silly giggle that sounded like a man who needed a longer rest on Kauai than he had originally had.

December 29, 1984: Lance has called me every day since our last meeting. I have suggested on several occasions that he see a psychiatrist for his personal problems. He declines, telling me that he is quite happy with his relationship with Dorie. Although it might seem ephemeral, she is more understanding than anyone he has ever been with in flesh and blood. I am truly concerned for his mental health.

January 4, 1985: At 2:30 a.m. there is a knock on my apartment door. Through a slight crack, I carefully ask who's there. A raspy, subdued voice answers, "Lance."

"Geez, it's 2:30, Lance," I answered.

He forces his way in and sits down. He looks terrible, but unusually calm. The wild look has left his eyes, but he seems drained of vitality. His cheeks are hollow, his skin swarthy. It is not the same man I had met a few weeks before at Zippy's. He looks at least 60 years old.

He asked me if I had the tape recorder handy. I said I did. Apparently recognizing the research value of his nightmares, he demanded that I record our conversation. This is Lance's verbatim statement:

"Dorie is not a dream, Dr. Grant. She's real. I know that sounds insane, but I first noticed it when I would wake up in the evening after dreaming of our lovemaking. The bed next to me would be warm, as if someone had been laying there. It occurred to me that during my dreams, when she touched me, it felt hot, like living flesh. This was no dream, it was truly a woman who embraced me. Hawaiians often talk about things that come into their rooms at night. I'm sure you've heard of the 'sickness' that they say they sometimes experience. Both men and women get it. In fact, when I was at Manoa, they said the dorms always had this 'sickness.'

"It starts when you feel someone is in the room with you and when you try to get up and look at who it is, they grab you by the neck or throat and start to choke you. They say it's like someone sucking your breath out or smothering you. I used to imagine the lips of a demon placed like a suction tube over your mouth, draining away your life. Europeans called them *incubus* or *succubus*. They said it was also a very sexual experience.

"I began to think about Dorie, Dr. Grant, and I thought maybe she was one of these spirits coming into my bed at night. Only, instead of choking me suddenly, she was slowly destroying me with these dreams. Look at me. I have no energy. I don't want to do anything, but wait for her to come when I'm asleep. Yeah, I know it's crazy, but I look forward to her coming. I don't fight the pressure on my chest and sucking on my mouth. I just let it go.

"Anyway, one night I woke up and not only found the spot

next to me warm. But there was a strand of black hair on the pillow. Here, see. Look at it. I measured it. It's at least 11 inches. It's too long to be mine. It was just laying there, like she wanted me to know that she was real, not a dream.

"So I got this plan from reading an old Japanese ghost story. I convinced myself that if I wanted to find out what Dorie really was, then I would need to get up during our lovemaking and not afterwards. If during the dream I could pinch myself, then I'd open my eyes and see her true form. So this evening I went to bed with this little pen knife. At the moment the dream began, I would poke myself with the knife and wake up.

"She's real, Dr. Grant. I did it. Look, the wound in my leg is still bleeding. It hurts, but at least I'm free of her. I've seen what she is, and now I know she'll never come back except to kill me.

"When the dream started, we were on the beach together, down near Ala Moana, and she was caressing me and telling me how happy I made her. She said that she wanted to meet my family and maybe one day she would be only mine. Her lips began to run up my neck and then firmly planted a kiss upon my mouth. Her mouth opened wide and began to suck the wind from my lungs—a gentle, loving motion that was far too pleasurable to be painful. I almost succumbed fully to her and one more night might have nearly given her whatever little of life I had in me. But my desire for survival must have overcome the temptation to submit, and I struck my leg several times with the knife I clutched in my hand. The pain was excruciating and my eyes were forced open, although I could not scream.

"It is impossible, Dr. Grant, to describe the hideous thing that I saw lying on my chest. It wasn't a cat, but a cat-woman, perhaps three-and-a-half feet long, stretched out upon me. In the darkness of my room I couldn't distinguish the face, except that it had a human mouth with the red-burning eyes of a demon.

"When our eyes met, the dream was lost. Her mouth was still upon mine, and the sucking became vicious, as if, in her exposure, she was going to kill me. I was so terrified I could do nothing but pray. She clawed, screeched and writhed like a rabid animal. She pulled her hairy body off of me and then leaped off the bed and vanished into the wall. I swear, Dr. Grant, it was a damn *obake neko*. I've heard about them. There was a plantation laborer killed by a damn cat spirit years ago. They found him scratched to death and his lungs collapsed. Blood all over his house. Neighbors said he killed some kittens and the *obake neko* got its revenge.

"I've thought about it Dr. Grant, and I guess all those animal dreams, it was like *pule anaana*—like someone praying me to death. All the dogs trying to get into me and in some crazy way this cat got sent. I'm sure someone wants me dead, someone is sending these things to me. Damn, if I just could figure out who and why.

"The nutty thing is, I think Dorie—or whoever she was— really did love me. She could have killed me, but she didn't. I remember the last look that horrible face gave me wasn't hate, but almost . . . well . . . desire."

After he finished relating that rather unbelievable tale, Lance thanked me for my friendship and wished me well. I've heard some strange fantasies before, but the *obake neko* of Kaimuki has to be one of the most bizarre. He did have evidence of the knife wound on his leg, but that proved nothing except that he was self-destructive, and there was the long strand of black, silky hair. I have not communicated with Lance in person since that night. I understand that he has changed his major and is slowly piecing his life back together. When he learned of my desire to write down these experiences, he sent me a brief note: "Dear Dr. Grant: Go ahead and tell the story. I've set all those things aside and I'm better for it. I'm certain that my imagination got carried away, although I'm still looking for a Dorie (ha ha). If others learn to stay away from poking their noses in all that stuff, I hope your article helps."

Unfortunately, I have discovered that "there are more things to heaven and earth than dreamed of in your philosophy," Lance. I wished I could explain it all away as imagination or psychic warp. The truth is, several months after the events described above, I was sleeping in my apartment when I began to feel a sensation, like something pressing me into the bed. I was laying on my stomach, so that I couldn't see what it was. At first, I thought someone was pulling a prank, but I couldn't even let a simple scream out of my mouth. Whatever it was on my back was somehow taking my breath away.

In the struggle to get up, I turned my head and looked into the face of an old Japanese woman lying full-length in bed with me. Her face was no more than five inches from mine and she was waiting to see my reaction. I couldn't scream, but I am certain my eyes revealed my terror. She gave me a sinister grin and then let out a cackle like an old, evil witch. At that moment she dematerialized next to me in the bed. The pressure also vanished and I could once again breathe. During the entire experience I was wide awake.

Who she was, or what connection she had with Lance's experience, I cannot say. But I believe that this should be my final article about the supernatural. As a wise man once said, it is better not to dabble with things demonically immense and unfathomable. I pray, dear reader, that you will never in the darkness of the night reach out to touch something that doesn't belong there. It may have plans for you.

Don't Step on my Grave: A Journey into Asian Terror

The drone of Japan Air Lines' Flight 71y helps me slip into an uneasy sleep, where brash images of grossly painted death masks greet me with their ghoulish, fixed grins. I stir out of the nightmare long enough to order one more Kirin from the solicitous, neatly starched stewardess, who would have probably avoided me like the plague if she had known but a tenth of my dreams.

I am hoping that this third beer will put me into a very deep sleep, far from the nightmarish faces. After taking a long, cooling swill of the brew, I pry myself out of the narrow economy seat and visit the last row to check on Eric and Lillian Kawafuchi. They make me very glad that my demons are largely restricted to my sleep.

Eric seems placidly absorbed in a copy of Wings magazine, but I can tell that he has but one thought—the well-being of Lillian. She is the only one of us, ironically, who seems able to sleep on the flight. She is warmly cuddled up in the airline blanket, looking in her sleep like she has no care in the world. Her peaceful face reveals her good-looking, Hawaiian-Chinese features. It's terrifying how much a beautiful countenance can be twisted, wrinkled and aged by fear. The Lillian Kawafuchi I had met two months earlier showed no trace of this resting angel.

I know this article was expected a lot sooner than this. And I know my editor will be surprised when he sees the return address postmarked Japan. I had been looking forward to this six-month sojourn to Japan for a long time, ever since I learned that I had been contracted to serve as a researcher/evaluator for the National Institute for Multimedia Education—the University of the Air program. But, in the last few weeks, so much has taken place that the best way to explain it is to start at the beginning—when I received that call from Lillian.

I can still remember the brittle voice on my answering machine at home. At first I was convinced that it was some kind of prank being played by a friend. After all, the timing was more than a bit coincidental—I had just gotten home from my monthly ghost tour of downtown Honolulu. But no actress, no matter how well-trained, could have added that touch of genuine hysteria that was clearly audible on the tape.

"Dr. Grant, my name is Lillian Kawafuchi. Please call me this evening, no matter how late. It is a matter of grave importance. I swear to you that I'm a responsible person. This is not a crank call. It involves a restless spirit. A life may be in danger."

As many of you readers may be aware, I am a collector of supernatural tales, lore and experiences. However, I have always had difficulty convincing people that I don't like investigating these phenomena on a first-hand basis. I have no philosophical or metaphysical foundation for my reluctance to practice psychic investigations or "ghostbusting." My reasons are far more basic— I am a coward. Anytime I have come close to mysterious sounds, phosphorescent lights, or disembodied spirits, my feet move quickly in the opposite direction. Consequently, I decided not to return the call.

Lillian Kawafuchi, however, was persistent. At about 11:30 p.m. she called again. I agreed to meet her the next morning at Zippy's coffee shop, near Washington Intermediate School. A public place in daylight, I figured, was about as safe an environment as I could find.

Although I had forgotten to ask her for her description, I realized the next morning that I didn't need one. Lillian was a 30-year-old woman who looked 60. If she ever was a stylish dresser, it didn't show that morning. She was wearing a yellow print muumuu that needed ironing, rubber slippers, and a look of fear. Around her neck was a large crucifix and in her hands she clutched a rosary. She wasn't wearing any make-up. And besides, the lines of tension on her face could not have been covered up. No eye shadow could have softened the dark circles and deep crow's feet that marred her once beautiful eyes. This was a woman with a serious mental problem who needed professional help, I thought to myself. Forget the ghost stuff.

When I heard her story over what seemed a dozen cups of coffee, I relaxed my first harsh judgment of her. Lillian Kawafuchi may have had emotional problems, but at her core she was a sane, rational human being who was attempting to understand and cope with a series of events that would have driven anyone to the edge.

"Last month, my husband, Eric, and his family observed the first-year memorial service for his father. My father-in-law was a successful businessman who at first disapproved of Eric's marriage to a non-Japanese girl. Eric and I had met in California when we were in college. Since his father was very old-fashioned about Eric marrying a Japanese girl, we eloped.

"The first year after we moved back to Hawaii, it was hard for Eric. We usually did things only with my family. But after our first son was born, Mr. Kawafuchi relaxed his objections somewhat. In fact, he told me before he died that he thought that Eric couldn't have found a better wife than me.

"Still, some of the relatives don't really like me. They think that Eric married below his station. So, when we went to the memorial services, a couple of them snubbed me. Not that I cared, but one of his aunts was real snotty. She even had the gall to tell me that Mr. Kawafuchi died with great bitterness because of Eric's elopement. I don't believe that because he told me that he liked me.

"After the services at the temple, I went with Eric, his mother, brother and sisters to father's gravesite at the Moiliili Japanese Cemetery. I'm Catholic, and I don't understand Buddhist things. I didn't know all those spooky things Japanese believe about the dead and graveyards. Now I know, but it's too late."

She started to cry, so I offered her my clean napkin. I thought about all the tidbits of information I knew about behavior in the graveyard: "Don't point at a grave," "Don't whistle in the graveyard." I thought about the hundreds of times I must have violated this rule or that without any repercussions for this "dumb haole."

"What do you think you did to cause your problems?" I asked.

"I stepped on his grave. So he's driving me insane."

I probably should have terminated the conversation at this point with some friendly advice to see her family doctor. As an aficionado of graveyards, I must have stepped on thousands of graves. The idea that some spirit is going to drive me insane for putting my foot above their little plot of ground is a concept that is far too superstitious for me to take too seriously. All that Lillian needed was strongly worded advice from a voice of authority.

"I'm not sure that stepping on a grave can really unleash a spirit's revenge, Lillian. You will find that many, many ghost occurrences are actually flights of the imagination," I admonished.

"You mean you don't believe that ghosts exist? You don't think that spirits can make communication with the living? You tell those ghost stories and you . . . "

I could see that she was crestfallen. But she had hit me at my weakest point. When a supernatural experience is related to me in which the events take place in the past and the haunting is resolved, I usually accept the facts and insights as legitimate. But when I am confronted with a person being haunted in the present, I always tend to leap to explanations of psychological disturbances, overactive imaginations, or weakmindedness.

My personal fear of losing control over what is real or unreal serves as a defense mechanism. I wanted to believe that Lillian was losing her grasp on reality due to some deeper mental health problem, not an angered spirit. Still, I didn't want her to lose confidence in my willingness to accept some other possible explanation for unusual phenomena.

"I do believe that there are larger mysteries around us and that sometimes we are blessed with a glimpse of another spirit realm. But, if we accept everything as supernatural, then we lose total balance."

"You think that I'm 'losing balance'?" she asked.

"I don't know, Lillian. Why don't you tell me why you think the spirit of your father-in-law is driving you insane."

"When I first stepped on the grave, my mother-in-law acted

all excited, like I had done something terrible. I hadn't done it intentionally. Because the graveyard is so damn small and tight, I placed my foot on the grave to get leverage to place a little offering on the tomb. Eric only laughed and told his mom not to be so superstitious. I apologized, and I thought that was that.

"But, two days later, terrible things started to happen. Eric and I have two sons—Dean, who is 5 years old, and Tommy, who's only 3. I work for the state as a systems analyst. After I get off work at 5 o'clock, I pick up the boys at my mom's house and then get home about 6 o'clock, the same time as Eric. Only this evening, Eric wasn't home. So I started dinner and went into the bedroom to take a quick shower.

"When I opened the towel closet, I saw on the floor a long, silver object that I know wasn't there that morning. I'm no expert on Japanese culture, but it looked like a real samurai sword.

"When Eric got home about an hour later, I asked him about the sword in the closet. He gave me a puzzled look, so I went to get it—only it wasn't there. I swear to you that I saw the sword. I touched it. It wasn't my imagination. Yet I tore the closet apart less than an hour later and it was nowhere to be found. Eric thought I was joking, but it was no joke. It really bothered me at work the next day. How could I imagine something so real?

"That weekend Eric and the boys went to Kanewai Park near the University. I was cleaning up the kitchen, sweeping out under the sink, when I found the sword again. I figured Eric was trying to hide it because it must have been expensive and he knew we couldn't afford it. So I brought it out from under the sink, put it on the kitchen table, and dug out all our bank statements from the last few months. I went over every one of them, Dr. Grant, and couldn't find any canceled checks or withdrawals that would cover the purchase of a samurai sword.

"A couple of hours later, when Eric returned home, I confronted him at the back door. Why was he trying to make me think I was crazy? I had found his damn sword and wanted to know how he could afford to buy it. What did he want with such a thing? The kids were all excited that Daddy had bought a sword. I told him I didn't approve and since when did he buy things without discussing it with me?

"When I went to show it to him, it wasn't on the table where I had left it. That's when I lost my temper and started throwing things and screaming. I was hysterical, Dr. Grant."

I haven't collected too many supernatural stories concerning samurai swords in Hawaii. There was the story I heard on Maui about a construction project on the site of an old Shinto shrine which had been demolished. Every time the workmen passed two ferns which had been planted on either side of the shrine's entrance, they felt a tingling sensation. Upon digging the plants up, they found under each fern carefully wrapped samurai swords that had evidently been buried following the attack on Pearl Harbor. I have also heard how the spirit of those killed by a sword stayed near the weapon as unhappy ghosts. But I never had I hear a tale about a disappearing sword.

"Was that the last time you saw this sword?"

"One other time I found it in the closet. This time I didn't tell Eric. I knew that it would only disappear. But I touched it. I pulled the blade out. Dr. Grant, there was blood dripping from it.

"That night, when Eric got home, I couldn't talk to him. He asked me how work was and I ignored him. Every time I looked at his face I wanted to scratch his eyes out. When we finally went to bed, he started to touch me. I slapped his face and went to sleep on the living room couch. When he followed me, I turned on him and kicked him in the chest so hard that he flew back against the wall. With my hands flying out of control, I gave him three hard blows to his head. He fell unconscious to the floor.

"Dean and Tommy heard the fight and got out of bed. They were screaming in fear. I only laughed. Eric was bleeding profusely from his nose and I bent over him and dabbed the red fluid as if it was harmless paint. I remember a pleasurable sensation as the warm blood stained my finger.

"I've never studied karate or kung fu, but Eric later said that my movements had been like a trained martial arts fighter. When he came to, he could see that I was terrified by what I had done. I think he was more frightened by my strange behavior than angry at me. The funny thing is that I've never felt remorse for hurting him. Even now, although I know it was wrong, I feel no guilt. All I can remember is the pleasure of the blood on my hands."

She said the last line so calmly that shivers went up and down my spine.

"The next morning I called in sick to work. I haven't gone back since. I can't think of anything except that stupid sword and the desire I have sometimes to hurt my family. They've taken Dean and Tommy away from me. I tried to drown Dean in our bathtub. I was bathing him and wanted to see how long it would take for him to stop breathing underwater. So I pushed his head down and just held it there as my little boy struggled in my grasp. If Eric hadn't heard the commotion, I would have killed my own son."

I thought of a dozen agencies to call that would give her psychological or spiritual counseling. But Lillian Kawafuchi had tried them all. Convinced that the spirit of her father-in-law had come back from the grave for some reason to drive her to murderous insanity, she had sought out priests, a *kahuna,* and every other kind of medium to relieve her possession. Some gave her comfort. Others gave her prayers. A few said that she needed medical help. Eric was hinting at committing her to a hospital. Glen Grant, I learned, was her last resort.

"What in the hell do you think I can do that the others haven't?" I asked.

"I think no matter how wild this all sounds, you believe me. I trust your advice. Tell me what to do to save my family, and I'll do it."

I agreed to meet Eric and to accompany her to a few spiritual counselors that I thought would release her from the "restless spirit." What I didn't tell her was that I was hoping to guide her to a psychiatric counselor.

"Thank you. There is one last thing that you should know, something I did a few days ago that even Eric doesn't know. I found myself sitting in the main terminal at the Honolulu International Airport. I don't remember how I got there. This was in my hand."

She showed me a one-way ticket to Tokyo. This young woman, I was convinced, was headed for the loony bin.

The Kawafuchi home is a pleasant, two-bedroom, concrete house in Manoa Valley just *mauka* of Manoa Park. A few months ago the house probably would have been filled with sounds of laughter, children playing, and the socializing of a young, upwardly mobile couple who loved each other very much. Now, the house is darkened and quiet, the curtains drawn. The idle toys are the only reminders of the two children who have been turned over to Eric's mother for safekeeping.

From the moment I met him, I could sense that Eric was hesitant to bring someone with my "*obake* reputation" into his family problems. He had first been harangued by relatives and friends to seek medical care for Lillian. He was under a lot of pressure to institutionalize her. Yet, in his heart, he wanted to believe that his wife wasn't crazy, that maybe the cause of her bizarre behavior was "supernatural," as she claimed. Eric was desperate to get his wife back to normal, even if it meant using, as he put it, a "ghostbuster."

He felt a little more reassured when I privately informed him that my goal was to eventually encourage his wife to seek psychiatric counseling once our supernatural ventures had failed.

Two nights later, with the help of friends in the Japanese American community, a private audience was granted to Lillian by one of Hawaii's most highly respected *odaisan*—the blind seer of Pauoa. The ceremony was unexpectedly short, as the agitated *odaisan* informed us as soon as we entered her incense-filled home that the young woman was in mortal danger. A spirit had possessed Lillian's body and soul, a spirit with revenge and death as its only thought.

We told her about Lillian having stepped on Eric's father's grave and the *odaisan* asked for any object that had belonged to Mr. Kawafuchi. Eric took off a family ring he had inherited and placed it in the blind woman's hand.

"This is not the spirit who seeks blood. Your father has crossed the bridge between life and death and finds contentment on the other side. The spirit who invades the woman has not crossed the bridge," she said.

"Who is it?" Eric asked.

"I cannot say. But she has stepped on his grave. He has found a way back to life through her."

66

About an hour later, at the request of the *odaisan*, we were hunting around a pitch-dark Moiliili graveyard, looking for a grave near Mr. Kawafuchi's that Lillian may have inadvertently desecrated. The flashlight in my hand was shaking. I watched very carefully where I put my feet.

There was a tomb next to Mr. Kawafuchi's which Lillian admitted she may have put her foot against when she leaned over with her offering.

It was very old and was inscribed in Japanese characters. Not understanding Japanese, we copied the characters down and went back to Pauoa where the *odaisan* was waiting in prayer.

"Tada," she interpreted the characters. "That is his name. This spirit has committed a horrible deed. It is bound to earth to relive its sin again and again until it finds atonement. The young woman is his vessel on earth. He will use her to commit his sin again."

"What did he do?" I asked as naively as possible, not necessarily wanting to know the answer.

"It is locked in his heart and will not be revealed until it is done. You must take this child with a priest to the place where the sin was committed. There you must pray for the soul to find peace and to cross the bridge. Then the young woman will be safe."

With the help of my good friend, Katsumi Onishi, I was able to translate other characters on the memorial tablet indicating that "Tada" had died in 1912. Using Board of Health records, it didn't take too long to learn that a Japanese immigrant by the name of Naoki Tada had been murdered by an unknown assailant on July 7, 1912.

Although the old Pacific Commercial Advertiser didn't cover crimes among the immigrants too closely, on microfilm I found one short reference in the July 8, 1912 edition to "an unusual Japanese death." The victim, unnamed in the account, had been found in Tin Can Alley, horribly dismembered.

The archives listed a Naoki Tada having arrived in Hawaii on July 6, 1912. He had been here less than one day when he had been murdered. The village of origin in Japan was listed as Gifu. When I showed my information to the Kawafuchis, Lillian started sobbing. The date of Tada's murder, July 7, was the same day as

Eric's father's death. She had put her foot against the tomb on the 77th anniversary of his murder.

Considering that he had been in the Islands only one day when he was murdered, Naoki Tada's sin had probably been committed in Japan. The crime that he was trying to run away from evidently caught up with him and left him in grisly pieces. I thought about that one-way ticket to Tokyo that Lillian had shown me and realized that this mystery wasn't going to be resolved in Hawaii.

For Eric and Lillian, their future hinges on pursuing this matter no matter what the cost or commitment of time. For myself, my first-ever trip to a country I've longed to visit is now terribly and strangely complicated by the added burden of helping two strangers to exorcise some restless ghost.

As Japan Air Lines 71y makes it final landing approach, I am now convinced that this could be a tragic waste of time and money. But my thoughts are on Lillian Kawafuchi, her turmoil and anguish. So far, I have given her some comfort and direction. I admit that I'm motivated by a slight messianic urge, but I sincerely want to help this woman.

I will write as soon as I can concerning Lillian's condition. Even now as I pen these final words, we are touching down in the land of the rising sun.

November 5—A Shrine in Inuyama Village, 11:00 (11 a.m.)

The small stone statue of Jizo, the protector of the departed spirits of children, stares at me from the corner of the little graveyard in the village of Inuyama. Around his neck he wears a dainty, red wool bib. On his head is a matching little cap. It seems so incongruous to see a gray stone statue so lovingly adorned in human dress. Centuries of his repose and gentle kindness caress me across a small inner court where children, wholly impervious to the sacredness of the site, play tag. I imagine the little god holding out the folds of his robe—saving from the fires of an eternal hell the tens of thousands of infants cast into an early grave— and my exhausted, depressed spirits seem lifted.

Eric is recovering well. The doctors say he can go home to Hawaii soon. Lillian? She seems to hardly remember anything that has happened. Of the three of us, she has an unsettling psychic calm that disturbs the hell out of me. They tell me that, after an exorcism, it's a natural condition. She's waiting for Eric to get back on his feet and then she says that life back in Hawaii will be better than ever. Hurrah.

This haven of peace in the bustle of Inuyama is the perfect place to sort out my notes and journal entries. I'm too tired to write it all out again in smoother fashion, so please tolerate the erratic jumps in chronology and choppy syntax. But I'm anxious to let your readers finally know the truth as faithfully as possible.

October 3—Hotel Ginza Ocean, Tokyo, 22:30 (10:30 p.m.)

After waiting two days in Tokyo, we have at last located an interpreter who will accompany us to the village of Gifu. Her name is Chieko Mizoue, a capable, attractive woman who is a professional interpreter for the Japan Tourist Organization. It is unusual to engage these types of services, we are told. The expense, therefore, is in proportion to the special treatment. But, if we are to unravel the mystery of Naoki Tada's death, and thereby release Lillian Kawafuchi from her fits of violence and mental anguish, it will take more than saying, "*Ohayoo gozaimasu. Ogenki desu ka?*" We have told Mizoue-san only that we are "looking up a little family history."

Eric has grumbled about the expenses, so I told him I'll take care of my own bills, plus help pay for Mizoue-san's fee. I'm beginning to see a side of Eric that I don't particularly like.

Lillian, on the other hand, has become so happy and relaxed, I'm ready to think her cured. The tension and worry from her face has disappeared, restoring her prettier features. She seems to relish every sight and sound in Tokyo as if she were a child in a toy store. *Gin-bura*, or Ginza cruising, has become a passion for her, although Eric is constantly reminding her that their budget doesn't allow for shopping at designer stores.

After dinner, a curious event. Lillian insists on having her face read by a *ninso*, a sidewalk fortune-teller, sitting behind a tiny table tucked in an alcove. It's almost comical the way this sober, middle-aged fortune-teller, looking more like your typical salaryman in a business suit than a seer, sits behind his yellow-glowing lantern waiting to divine the mysteries from the dimple in your cheek or curve of your nose. Since Eric wouldn't shell out the few hundred yen, I treat Lillian, who insists that I get my face read first. The *ninso* points his flashlight directly in my face, stares at my oversized nose and rattles off some nonsense in broken English about irresponsible, unrealistic and poor—all of which I already knew. Then he swings the flashlight into Lillian's face, lets out a long, concerned expulsion of air between his teeth and gives me back my yen!

"Sorry. Cannot read. Sorry. Take money back."

Then he packs up his sidewalk shop and rushes off through the crowds as if he was late for a bus. I can see this has greatly affected Lillian. Despite the protests of both Eric and myself, she believes the *ninso* read something terrible in her fortune. We try to cheer her up by taking in the sights of Roppongi, but to no avail. She is anxious to get to Gifu, so we make reservations on the Shinkansen, which leaves tomorrow at 8 a.m. from Tokyo Station.

October 4—On the Bullet Train to Nagoya, 9:15 a.m.

Fuji-san appears through the gray haze as a large painted backdrop from the window of the world's fastest train that doesn't seem to be moving quite as fast as I would have imagined at 250 kph. At breakfast, Eric seemed more sullen than usual, while Lillian's anxieties from the *ninso* incident seemed to have vanished. She and Mizoue-san have become fast friends, occupying adjacent seats on the train and talking about "America Containing Japan," the current topic of conversation everywhere in this country.

I have poured through paperback editions of Lafcadio Hearn's "Unfamiliar Glimpses of Japan" and "Japan: An Attempt at an Interpretation," trying to better understand some of the cultural background to Japanese religious beliefs concerning spirits of the dead. Although I have collected the ghostlore of Hawaii's people for nearly 15 years, I've never read Hearn with clearer appreciation than this morning, cutting across an island nation so enigmatic to Westerners. "The land where the dead rule;" "ghosts of the ancestors are everpresent;" "the spirits never rest until their honor is restored."

I keep trying to imagine the Honolulu police back on July 7, 1912 finding the remains of Naoki Tada in Tin Can Alley. "Dis-

70

membered," the newspaper had said. I wondered if that was a euphemism for the descriptions given by Lafcadio Hearn of the revenge meted out against *hinin*, or outcasts. These wandering pariahs, "not human beings," had perpetrated a grave dishonor and would sometimes by hunted down by an avenger and hacked to death with a sword until all that was left was an unrecognizable lump of human mincemeat. A shiver runs through me whenever I imagine that horrendous sight.

Otherwise, it is a delightful ride to Nagoya. I notice that Lillian laughs now. A very infectious laughter.

October 4—Gifu City Hotel, Midnight

Gifu is a great disappointment. Maybe I was expecting some rural cluster of blue-tiled oriental roofs near fields of rice being harvested by quaintly dressed farmers. Why do I keep infusing Japan with images stolen from a pre-Meiji feudal world?

Flattened by American bombers, Gifu is now an ugly city of tall buildings, narrow alleyways exploding in neon, bright red streetcars, and gray, gray, everywhere gray.

Lillian and Mizoue-san make the best of a dismal situation by forcing us men to go to a karaoke bar. Eric bows out, complaining of a headache, so the three of us go drinking and singing. Lillian has a great voice, even if the songs are all in Japanese except for "New York, New York" and "Country Roads."

October 8—Gifu City Hotel, 15:00 (3 p.m.)

Lillian and I have become quite close during this ordeal that is actually turning into a very pleasant vacation. She tells me that Eric can brood if he wants, but she already feels cured. In fact, the whole ghost nonsense back in Honolulu seems like a dark fantasy. The four of us have been spending the days sightseeing as much as possible, savoring the myriad of sights that all seem so neatly packaged like a *teishoku* platter. Eric finally forces us back into reality. The crime of Naoki Tada has to be discovered, the scene of the horror revisited, and the spirit's anguish released.

Mizoue-san, still believing that we are simply compiling an accurate family tree, assists us in examining the city records. No luck. They were all destroyed in the bombing raids on Gifu. Then we start visiting the various neighborhood shrines and graveyards, looking for a Tada family marker, hoping relatives are still in the area. It's more impossible than looking for a needle in a haystack.

Finally, Mizoue-san has a brilliant idea. She'll go back to Tokyo and contact the National Archives. Every immigrant leaving the nation would have needed to contract with an immigrant labor company operated under government sanction. Perhaps Naoki Tada's contract would indicate more about his family background. Working through the Japanese governmental bureaucracy, we are warned, may take a long while.

October 22—Gifu City Hotel, 14:30 (2:30 p.m.)

Nearly two weeks have passed and we still haven't heard from Mizoue-san. The sightseeing has become tedious, so I spend the long days with a novel or watching the rains fall on Gifu. I'm saving money by dining on *ramen* and *gyoza*. Charles Tuttle must love me. I've spent thousands of yen buying up his Japan books. Eric and I had a slight blowout two nights ago. He said I had taken them on this wild goose chase and he'd lose his job if he didn't get back to Hawaii. I told him that it wasn't *my* wife who called him . . . and if he didn't like it, he could go back to Honolulu or to hell as far as I was concerned. We later apologized to each other, but I've noticed that we don't talk much anymore.

Lillian has been having funny mood swings. A few times I caught her with an expression on her face that resembled that unhappy creature sitting across from me at Zippy's a couple of months ago. But most of the time she's bubbling over with good spirits and optimism. Every afternoon she goes to a small Japanese garden, where she meditates.

Last night, after Eric went to bed early, she and I went to a small grill for a couple of beers. The smoke from the *tori* and *tako* sizzling over the charcoal was like opium and we went from Sapporo beer to *sake* to Japan's *okolehao*, a great poison called *shochu*. I guess you could say we were drunk. At one point she reached across the table, took my hand in hers and told me that she was very grateful for all I had done. Instinct told me to take my hand back, but the *shochu* stopped me. Instead, I said some things I shouldn't have, but I'm now convinced that the real problem with Lillian Kawafuchi doesn't have to do with stepping on the grave of Naoki Tada. It is simply the result of a very unhappy marriage.

October 24—Gifu City Hotel, 23:00 (11 p.m.)

Mizoue-san showed up this afternoon with a photocopy of Naoki Tada's immigration contract. While he had listed Gifu as his place of origin on the Hawaii records, it was clear from the Japanese contract that he was born and raised in the village of Inuyama, about 45 minutes away on the private Meitetsu train line. Mizoue-san thinks we'll have better luck there tracing the Tada line, since it is a relatively smaller and more rural village than Gifu.

I have mixed feelings about proceeding. Lillian seems so "normal" that stirring up this ghostly business may only cause her to revert to her earlier condition. In addition, Eric and I are not on the best of terms. In fact, he suggested at dinner that if I want to cut out, I can. Almost in spite of him, and to escape Gifu, I'm putting on a happy face. "Naw, let's go and get it over with," I told him.

October 27—Inuyama Ryokan, 20:30 (8:30 p.m.)

Tada is a well-known name in Inuyama. Masatake Tada owns the largest fish market; Takashi Tada drives the fastest taxi. Rico Tada sells small *omamori* to tourists at the entrance to Inuyama-jo, the oldest original wooden castle in Japan that sits high above the Kiso River. Shigeru Tada operates one of the river rafts that takes visitors down the Kiso River rapids, and "Suzy" Tada takes visitors down another kind of rapids. We talked to them all and none knows of, or admits to knowing the name of, Naoki Tada. A Tada family also operates the small *ryokan* in which we are staying. It's located along the edge of Inuyama, overlooking the Kiso River, and is cheap enough for our dwindling budget. Yesterday, Mizoue-san admitted that, although she has had fun trying to solve this mystery (and she has been gracious enough to do most of this work without pay!), she gives up. "This Tada must have had no relatives," she told me.

It was time for the truth, so I invited her to dinner at one of the finer Inuyama restaurants. It cost me nearly 30,000 yen, but I figured it was the least we owed Mizoue-san. When she heard about Lillian's spirit possession, the problems back in Hawaii, the murder of Tada and why we were in Japan, I figured she'd think us crazy. Call it a farewell dinner.

I was totally surprised by her response. Instead of being frightened off, she was more excited than ever by what she called "the *obake* hunt." No wonder no one admitted knowing Naoki Tada, she explained. If he had become a *hinin* due to some crime he had committed, then he no longer existed. He would have been purged from family records and the collective memory. But the crime, the crime would live on in the gossip of the old people. "We must look for the crime, Grant-san, not the criminal."

Then, with great embarrassment, Mizoue-san turned the subject to Lillian. They had become very close in the last few weeks. She was surprised when I described her violent behavior in Hawaii, since she had been so passive during her visit to Japan. In fact, Mizoue-san noted, it was almost like Lillian had come home, she was so at ease. In an uncharacteristically bold manner, she asked me if I liked Lillian as someone more than a friend.

I couldn't answer that question honestly. I told her I don't know. She told me that Eric thinks something's going on. Eric is an ass, I answered. It's no one's business how I feel. I've done nothing wrong.

October 29—Inuyama Ryokan, 18:30 (6:30 p.m.)

The first pieces of a jigsaw puzzle are always the hardest to match. When the pattern emerges, though, the solution always comes at a furious pitch.

Mizoue-san and I have left Lillian and Eric pretty much alone to patch up their marriage while we visit the Inuyama Community Welfare Center. The center sponsors daily activities for the senior citizens, so we have an opportunity to "talk story" with the old-timers. This girl is great at getting the stories out of the old folks. If I wasn't so preoccupied with getting the truth about Tada, I'd be overwhelmed with the richness of these lives and the abundance of tales that lead me into another world.

One spry, talkative *oba-chan* with a sharp memory starts to piece in the puzzle. She looks maybe 75 years old, but she tells us that last August she celebrated her 96th birthday. She has lived in Inuyama all her life, she explains, except for the year she spent in Kyoto studying the *shamisen*. Her father, a merchant with a love for refinement, had groomed her to become an excellent wife. She'll never forget when she returned to Inuyama. It was during the winter of 1912. The first snows had begun to fall, covering the village in a dreary whiteness. When her family and many friends greeted her at the train station, she asked for Fumiko, her dearest friend from secondary school. She had expected to see Fumiko carrying her little son Sunao at the station. In her last letter, she had promised to be there.

Her mother took her aside and whispered that Fumiko and Sunao were dead. Her husband had lost his mind one night. First drowning his little son in the well, he then put his blade through Fumiko before the shrine at the castle Inuyama-jo. The devil then disappeared from the earth. She remembers how her tears melted the snow that fell from her face as the whistle of the departing steam engine pierced the village air.

Oba-chan is crying as she tells us her story. Who was her husband, Mizoue-san asks. The name she can't (or won't) remember. But Fumiko's younger brother is still alive in Inuyama. He owns a little antique shop in the heart of the village, not far from Inuyama-jo. Maybe he'll remember.

When we returned to the *ryokan*, Lillian was getting back from a boat excursion on the Kiso River. She and Eric had had a long discussion about their marriage, her problems, and his feelings about what has happened. It evidently wasn't too pleasant. He went off sightseeing to Seti, 30 minutes to the north, and she went boat-riding. We told her about Oba-chan and that we may be close to uncovering the truth.

An hour later, Lillian visited me in my room. She seemed disturbed that Mizoue-san and I had been gone so long. Was I interested in Chieko, she asked. If anything happens between her and Eric, will I be there to help her? I got the most uncomfortable feeling I was supposed to do something right that moment, but I backed away, mumbled "sure," reassured her that we'd talk later, and that she'd better leave my room. I broke out in a cold sweat.

October 28—Inuyama Ryokan, 22:00 (10 p.m.)

This morning Lillian insists that she join Mizoue-san and me when we visit Naomichi Komanoya, Fumiko's brother. His antique store is on a narrow street about one kilometer from the tourist bustle of Inuyama-jo. It's a large, cluttered establishment, with cabinets of old lacquered bowls, ceramic vases and plates under protective glass, stacks of old, yellowed newspapers tucked in every corner, a 1987 calendar hanging on one wall, an old hand-colored print of a uniformed Emperor Meiji on another, and a rusty bicycle parked in the middle of an aisle.

We open the sliding glass door to the store and an old man with a cigarette dangling from his mouth, glasses brought down to the tip of his nose, and a newspaper in hand pokes his head through curtains that conceal a little side room where I can see a small television blaring a Tokyo quiz show. It's Komanoya-san.

Mizoue-san, using her most polite, subtle tone, introduces us as *gaijin* who are interested in a man who once lived in Inuyama before immigrating to Hawaii. His name was Naoki Tada.

I watched closely to see if the name meant anything to the old man. He took a puff from the cigarette, waved us off with the brush of a hand, muttered something in Japanese and turned away to his room. Having been so brusquely dismissed, we returned to the street, when we heard a hushed *"moshi-moshi"* coming up behind us. A courtly old man, sporting a thin moustache in the Errol Flynn tradition and bedecked in a colorful *yukata*, ran up to us in several short steps, his wooden *geta* sounding like the clops of a horse on pavement. He and Mizoue-san spoke for several minutes and then he led us off a few blocks through a charming lane of wooden houses to a large neighborhood shrine and graveyard. A few minutes later, we were standing before the dozens of wooden *ihai* (memorial marker) of Fumiko and Sunao Tada, the mother and child murdered 79 years ago.

Mizoue-san later explained that the old man was Fumiko and Naomichi's cousin, a former Tokyo cook, salesman, entertainer, *sake* brewer and just about anything else it took to survive in the hard years before and after the war. His name was Tokumaru Komanoya and his life in Tokyo had left him with a cosmopolitan air unlike his country cousin. He had returned to Inuyama, the village of his youth, 10 years ago and now spends afternoons playing cards or drinking whiskey with his cousin. He had been in the side room when he heard us talking about Tada. The Tokyo years had taught him that all men are a little evil and that enough shame had been borne since that fateful day.

We have filled Eric in on all the new information. He seems very moody after having spent another day at Seti, but he admits he's relieved that the ordeal may be over. All we need to do now is find a priest who is willing to help us. We want to perform the exorcism as soon as possible.

October 30—Inuyama Ward, Police Headquarters, 1:00 (1 a.m.)

My hands are still a little unsteady, but I want to scribble these memories down as fast as I can. The police have called the American Embassy in Tokyo for verification of our identities, passports, etc. So I may have to stay here the entire night. I don't know where the hell Lillian is, although I suspect she's with Eric. Mizoue-san is a nervous wreck. I've apologized for all this mess, but she says it was her own choice. At least she can still laugh.

After we learned the truth of Tada's heinous crime, we sought out an exorcist to help cleanse the spirit. But none of the official priests in the village would help us. Mizoue-san explained that they may have suspected the *gaijin* of being insincere or perhaps they thought it was all a hoax. So with her nose for getting information, Mizoue-san was able to locate a middle-aged couple who lived near the Inuyama train station who had the gift to perform *toritsu-banashi*—the evocation of the dead.

Mr. and Mrs. Sunoh didn't look like spiritual mediums of the table-tipping genre. Instead, they resembled the thousands of simple country folk that you saw daily in the prefecture. Yet, in their home was a remarkable miniature shrine, scores of small statuettes, burning candles, fragrant incense and paraphernalia beyond description. They listened patiently as Mizoue-san told our story and the advice that the *odaisan* of Pauoa Valley had given us.

Mr. Sunoh explained to us that the ritual of *toritsu-banashi* was very dangerous. The soul called back from the dead would find itself in great torment and confusion in the world of the living. And, on their return to the spirit realm, they would be in a lower state of spiritual progress. But Tada was unresolved in his madness. His hatred and violence intruded even now on the living. Whatever the risks, it would have to be done soon or the cycle of horror would recommence in one full revolution.

77

"Revenge is a most terrible emotion," added Mrs. Sunoh. "It leaves the spirit without understanding of life or death."

The site for the ceremony was to be the shrine below the castle Inuyama-jo, the very place where Tada had murdered his wife. We would need to wait until after the castle and nearby tourist sundry shops and restaurants closed. We agreed to meet at 22:00 (10 p.m.). Then the Sunohs excused themselves—they had to prepare for the ritual.

The rest of us returned to the *ryokan* to catch up on our rest. I tried to make peace with Eric, but he brushed me off and took a walk down to the river. Lillian said she needed to be alone and went off to her room. Since that afternoon, when she confessed her marriage was falling apart, Lillian had been unusually reserved with me. I wasn't sure whether it was because she was jealous of Mizoue-san, resolved to patch things up with Eric, or resentful that I hadn't made some kind of commitment. I tried to take a nap, but every time I shut my eyes I saw those silly death masks swizzing around me like gnats.

You can't keep any secrets in a small village. When we all rendezvoused at Inuyama-jo, Naomichi Komanoya was waiting for us. I couldn't tell whether the redness in his face was from drink or anger. He literally spit out his words to Mizoue-san and the Sunohs. They quietly responded and then he stormed off down the street to his shop.

"He doesn't want us to do this," Mizoue-san translated. "'Let the bastard burn in hell,' he told the Sunohs. But they said that the innocent will suffer if the dead are not made peaceful."

A crescent moon shone beautifully in the sky as we climbed the few dozen stairs into the shrine area where the murder had been committed. As we passed through one of the *torii* gates, I heard the sweet sounds of a *koto* being played in a nearby home. Here was the first time that I could actually feel the beauty that underlies the ugly excitement, surge and noise of modern Japan, and I was on my way to a conference with the dead. How appropriate.

The Sunohs had prepared the entire area. *Tatami* mats were carefully spread out and an array of soft lanterns illuminated the otherwise dark night. A cool breeze passed through us and the lanterns flickered and swung from their poles. We all took off our shoes and knelt on the mats, while the Sunohs placed before us three *ihai* with the names of the deceased on them. Fumiko's and her son's had been brought from their graves. Tada's had been made that afternoon by Mr. Sunoh. Candles and incense were burning before each, while the mediums donned pure white ceremonial robes secured with brilliant red sashes.

The purification sutras and offerings of uncooked rice and flowers to Tada's *ihai* seemed to last for hours. My knees and feet were numb and my patience to sit perfectly still was ready to collapse. I looked across at Lillian. She seemed as beautiful and serene as the *koto* music wafting up from the village below. A very jealous Eric was staring at me, and I decided that later I would tell him that I loved his wife and to hell with him. I couldn't help but feel a big smile come across my face, the smile you get when you outsmart an opponent at checkers. You could almost see him grinding his teeth.

"Tada! Tada! *Kitazo yo! Kitazo yo!*"

It was Mr. Sunoh, calling out loudly as if to someone standing on the other side of the graveyard. In his left hand he held an instrument shaped like a bow. Everytime he called out, he struck it loudly against his empty right hand. I asked Mizoue-san what he was saying. She said in a whisper, "I have come."

Again and again he called out the name of Tada, intoning almost in an hypnotic chant those eerie words, *"Kitazo yo! Kitazo yo!"* Mrs. Sunoh bowed very low to the mat and let out a high-pitched sing-song of *"Kitazo yo!"* that sent the shrill of death through my bones. I can't explain why, but hot tears streamed down my face as the two mediums maintained their harmony for the ghost of the murderer.

Mrs. Sunoh was now crawling and writhing all over the mat, her voice tortured in pain, her tone sinking lower and lower until the *"Kitazo yo!"* was no longer coming from her but from the man who had destroyed so many lives. Mrs. Sunoh looked up from the mat, her posture like a cat ready to pounce. The features of her face in the lantern illumination were distorted with rage.

A flood of hatred poured out of her mouth, spitting and snarling in madness. Mizoue-san, kneeling beside me, was shaking uncontrollably as she tried to translate.

"'Quickly, quickly,' he is saying, 'for I am in pain. I have no time. What do you want? What do you want? Great is the pain.'"

Mr. Sunoh now began to speak to the spirit. He asked it why it had come to inflict unhappiness on the innocent.

The voice from Mrs. Sunoh was gutteral and deadly. As the spirit spoke through her, Mrs. Sunoh's eyes seemed to fixate on me.

"She is not innocent," Mizoue-san translated. "She has betrayed me. Her body in hell feeds the worms and maggots. Her breasts are feasted upon by the cadaverous gods, her blood drunk by vultures. Her lover shall join her tonight."

With that, a dark laughter filled the air as Mrs. Sunoh collapsed, Mr. Sunoh and Mizoue-san rushing to her aid. I turned back to Lillian and Eric, who had been unearthly still during the ritual. Lillian seemed quite untouched by it all, her eyes gently closed with a sweet, childish smile on her face. Eric was gone.

I gently shook Lillian, trying to arouse her from her stupor, when she looked very lovingly at me and whispered, "I love you." She brought her face up close to mine and, as we pressed lips, I could again hear the soft *koto* music restore the serenity to the shrine. It was all over, and she belonged to me. I had won and her lips tasted so sweet that my eyes closed to imagine us far away from Inuyama, Tada and Eric.

When she broke away, I felt a gnat buzz my lips and trap itself in the saliva. I brushed it out with my finger and, looking down, saw that it was actually a grain of the uncooked rice used in the ritual. How in the hell did it get there, I thought, as I noticed it move a little on my finger.

"What in the hell?" I said to Lillian, holding it up in front of her. "Look at this."

She seemed uninterested and came forward to give me another kiss, when I noticed the same little rice grains were on her lips. Several of them started oozing out of her mouth, which I now saw was filled with the little white grains.

"Lillian?"

In the lantern's glow, I saw that they weren't grains of rice. They were living maggots eating the soft inner folds of her mouth. An open sore on the right side of her cheek was infested with them as strips of flesh peeled like silk from her face.

I gagged and pulled back as she lurched towards me, groping, whining how much she loved me. My skin recoiled from the cadaverous touch of her foul-smelling, rotted hands.

Throwing her off, I bolted back from the *tatami* mat just in time to see Eric step out from behind a small wall. He was carrying a bag from which he pulled a long, black object. The blade was tempered steel that flashed as he swung it up over his head. Tada's twisted hatred was in his eyes. He was muttering under his breath, seething with jealousy. As he stalked me back against the shrine, I was too frightened to move. All I can remember is shutting my eyes tightly and waiting for the blow that would send me to hell.

Mizoue-san told me later that it all happened so quickly that she and the Sunohs were too frozen to respond. I had let out a terrible scream, scrambling away from Lillian, who was still trying to hug me. Eric, wielding a samurai sword, had come at me when, suddenly, old Mr. Komanoya appeared from nowhere, plunging a small kitchen knife into Eric's thigh, sending him and the sword flying.

"I killed him once, many years ago," he explained to us through Mizoue-san. "I followed the mad dog to Hawaii and took revenge for my sister and nephew. I told you not to speak of Tada. Now his evil is like a plague on your house, also."

Lillian, who now appeared quite normal, was in mild shock, so we wrapped her up in a blanket from the Sunohs' car. Then we put a bandage on Eric's leg to stop the bleeding. He was in a daze, not knowing where he was or what he had just tried to do. We were going to get him to the village hospital, when Mrs. Sunoh started her *"Kitazo yo!"* chanting. I told Mizoue-san to tell her that we had had enough that night, when a powerful wind blew through the shrine, dowsing the candles and lanterns and casting us into an unearthly darkness. *"Kitazo yo! Kitazo yo!"* she continued, only this time her voice was high and gentle like a child's.

"I have come! I have come!" Mizoue-san translated. "My father has placed me in a dark hell, beyond even the reach of Jizo. He has sent my innocent mother to be a feast for flesh-eating gods. So great is his hatred, we cannot find light."

"Why is he so tormented?" asked Mr. Sunoh.

"Does he seek to kill me?" asked Komanoya-san.

"The man who dishonored my mother and cast us into pain is the man he wishes to kill. This man seduced my mother into sin and then fled before my father's sword. He cannot rest until his jealousy is satisfied."

The voice of Mrs. Sunoh became childish and pitiful. An overwhelming sadness filled us.

"Father, I forgive you for sending me to this torment. But I want to cross over to play with the children. Release me to be with my god Jizo."

I didn't see it, but Mizoue-san claimed that a large fireball, or *hinotama*, appeared above the graveyard following Sunoh's plea to his father. It glowed a bright yellow, swirled above the hundreds of tombs and then shot up and across Inuyama village, leaving a faded trail like a falling star.

November 6—Inuyama, Postscript.

The above notes, taken from my travel journal, explain the many events of last month. As I review them, I feel greatly embarrassed by the highly personal tone that grew in my feelings for Lillian Kawafuchi. Mr. Sunoh has explained to me that they were not my feelings, but the cycle of jealousy and revenge which Tada's possession of Lillian generated. He was trapped in a hell of his own making because he had not fulfilled the duty of his obligation. When the man seduced his wife, he was obliged to not only take her life, but the life of her lover. Then Tada could commit *seppuku* with honor. Not wishing for his son to be an orphan, he sent him to the other world to live with spirit children.

Only, he failed in his duty. He evidently had followed the adulterer to Hawaii, but his wife's brother, believing Tada to be a despised *hinin*, had cut him down before the vengeance could be satisfied. If Komanoya-san had known the truth about his sister's seduction, he would have viewed Tada's actions as honorable, not criminal.

Is Tada's spirit still filled with hatred? We think not. The morning after the *toritsu-banashi*, the old courtly cousin, Tokumaru Komanoya, was found dead in his bed. The coroner surmised he had died of a heart attack in his sleep. But the rumor in the village is that on his face was a frozen look of horror, as if a very old sin had finally caught up with him.

I heard that Lillian and Eric will be leaving for Hawaii in two days. They both seem very happy and look forward to picking up their lives with their two children in their perfect little Manoa Valley house. Eric apologized for nearly dividing me in half. The samurai sword? He had bought it in Seti and then stashed it in the bushes near the shrine that afternoon before the ritual. If I had read the guide books more carefully, I'd have suspected something fishy about his visits to Seti—it is the swordmaking center of Japan.

Mizoue-san went home to Tokyo, thanking me for such an exciting adventure, and I have decided to stay a few more days in Inuyama before taking on my responsibilities for the next six months in Chiba. The Oba-chan saw me sitting in the graveyard yesterday and sat next to me for a while. We couldn't communicate, but something in her eyes tells me she is grateful that her old friend Fumiko can now find salvation from her sins.

And I find great pleasure in the statues of Jizo. I sometimes think of Sunao in the eternal playground of children playing *jan-ken-po* or tag, watched over by this gentle god with the Mona Lisa smile.

Or I think of Lillian under the crescent moon, a night lulled by *koto* music in the lonely, beautiful shadow of Inuyama-jo castle, and I plan, over and over again, how, one day, I will get her back.

On the Kwaidan Trail of Lafcadio Hearn

e stepped into a narrow and dark cobblestone alleyway that wound through the heart of the fishing village of Mionoseki. The path opened up to a larger road lined with small, two-story wooden buildings that must have been standing one hundred years ago, when *he* walked through the village. Kajitani-sensei was scurrying up ahead, reading back to me from his dog-eared copy of "Glimpses of Unfamiliar Japan" passages he felt most appropriately captured the timelessness of this ancient village along the coast of the Sea of Japan:

"Mionoseki is so tightly pressed between the sea and the bases of the hills that there is only room for one real street; and this is so narrow that a man could anywhere jump from the second story of a house upon the water-side into the second story of the opposite house upon the land-side. And it is as picturesque as it is narrow, with its awnings and polished balconies and fluttering figured draperies."

There was little straining of the imagination to see the narrow street just as it had appeared in the hundred-year-old description. The concrete that had inundated the rest of the nation following the devastation of World War II had not yet found its way into Mionoseki. A comforting sense of solace that flows from things old filled a spirit unruffled by the few anomalies of television antennae, automobiles and neon signs that intruded upon the scene. Yes, he *must* have seen it just like this.

Two cherub-faced, blue-uniformed schoolboys not more then 10 years old came skipping towards us down the road, gleefully swinging their schoolbags. They suddenly stopped dead in their tracks, gaping at the *gaijin* towering over them.

"Peace," they said with huge grins, flashing the "V" symbols with their stubby little fingers. They laughed when I returned their greeting and then they scooted off a few doors down, turning into one of the old fish stores, where a monstrous dried *tako*, full-bodied with dangling tentacles, hung from the broad doorway.

"Grant-sensei, come. Come." It was Sekita-san signaling us to follow her up the hill behind the village to the Shinto shrine Miojinja. I had first met Kaoru Sekita, an archivist at Waseda University, through Noriko Nakamura, my research assistant at the University of the Air, where I was working temporarily in Tokyo. The three of us had quickly become somewhat of a team, exploring Tokyo districts night and day so that the American, they explained, could see the real Japan. Through her connections with scholars such as Dr. Kajitani, who lived in Izumo, Sekita-san had arranged our special three-day excursion to the province of the gods.

As a "tour guide," she was more comparable to a whirlwind than an escort. A full day with Sekita-san at the helm usually meant visiting at least a half-dozen shrines for the obligatory photograph and *omiyage*, five-minute tours of historical museums along the way, and gulping down bowls of *udon* as we raced to those "scenic" outlooks that more often were vistas of industrial destruction than natural wonder. Still, Nakamura-san and I always raced after our beloved Sekita-san, knowing full-well that somewhere along the way she would lead us into a genuinely unique experience that even many Japanese had never sampled. As we now followed her to Miojinja, I heard in the distance the faint beating of a *taiko* drum accompanied by the steady chant of a priest. Gathering before the temple's open entrance, still slightly panting from our uphill race, we stepped into a scene that certainly had been lifted out of Old Japan. The Shinto priest was in ancient costume, sitting on his *zabuton*, tapping the ceremonial drum in harmony with the movements of a beautiful young girl with long, black hair, wearing a pure-white gown decorated with an orange-red sash. Her movements were carefully measured, almost in slow-motion across the *tatami* mats of the temple floor, gracefully honoring the gods of this historic shrine.

"*Mika*, Grant-sensei. You very lucky."

"Mika? " I queried.

"A virgin of the shrine," Nakamura-san explained. "We are so fortunate that we came at this hour so that you could see her dance. This is very special."

A light rain sprinkled upon us as we silently watched the *mika* go through her paces, moving through space almost as if she were submerged in an underwater ballet. The ghost of ancient Nippon was brushing my shoulder, enticing me to sink into the *mika's* shadowy other world in which she had become entranced, and I wished the moment were without end. How far I had journeyed to savor this treasured vision, and I wondered if he had felt the same strange, spiritual stirring that, somehow, in his distant, alien world, so far removed from the land of my birth, I had mysteriously returned home.

Kwaidan, or uncanny tales, are usually filled with the frightening *obake* of our imaginations. The ghosts are apparitions and ghouls revenging murders, or lonely wraiths who haunt their sad corners of the earth. What would a supernatural tale be without special effects or poltergeist manifestations? We search so ardently for the tangible evidence of spirit, that we ignore the signs of the spiritual that frequently filter in and out of our lives with the silent grace of a *mika* dancer.

Only now, many months after returning to Hawaii, have I come to fully realize that during my brief six months in Japan I had been involved in a subtle, but mysterious, ghost story. Of course, I had not gone to Japan with the intentions of conducting ghost story collections or searching out *obake*. My appointment as a foreign researcher at the University of the Air had absolutely no connection with psychic or folklore research. Yet, from my first day in Japan, I can see that the hand of an old ghost had reached out across time, setting off a chain of events that would, by the day of my departure, leave its fingerprints upon my soul. As I indicated, it started on the very first day of my job. Although I had been invited to the university to conduct a very specific research project, I wasn't on the job for two hours when I realized that foreign researchers were also expected to have several private research projects. Quite frankly, since this was to be my very first trip to Japan and I spoke nary a word of the local lingo, I figured I'd be spending most of my free time struggling through *Nihongo*. So I was wholly unprepared when I was asked by a Japanese colleague, "What is your *personal* research, Grant-sensei?" Suffering a momentary brain spasm, but not wanting to lose face, I confidently shot back, "I am here to study Lafcadio Hearn."

Don't ask me where that came from—it just popped out of my mouth. Before the week was over, it popped out of my mouth at least a dozen more times, so that now it seemed generally true. To convince everyone that I was serious, I prowled through the small, English section of the school library, checking out every volume it contained of Hearn's writings, such as, "In Ghostly Japan," "Kwaidan," "Japan: An Interpretation," "The Romance of the Milky Way." Whenever the door to my office knocked, I would be sure to be holding a copy of one of his books in my hand, looking engrossed in an academic way. Hungry as I was for the English language, I would pour through Hearn's writings, comparing his experiences in Japan against mine, feeling humbled by the graceful power this Greek-British-American author had over the English language and practicing scholarly erudite comments just in case I was ever seriously asked how my research was progressing.

One afternoon I caught the subway into Tokyo, to Jena's Ginza bookstore, so I could purchase Hearn's first major work on his adopted country, "Glimpses of Unfamiliar Japan." My copy of that extraordinary work was kept forever in my knapsack wherever I traveled—indeed, I planned my weekend itineraries so I could duplicate his travels. At the village of Hase, in the presence of the great Daibutsu, I scribbled my impressions of the giant Buddha in the margins of the book alongside his own comments written one hundred years before. At the island of Enoshima, I gulped down a Kirin in a small inn, my Hearn faithfully in hand as I watched the "witchery" of a Japanese sun set, a fiery red ball sinking into a vividly blue ocean, the crimson rays shooting across the sea in replication of the old Japanese flag.

With Hearn as my guide, I fell in love with Jizo, the benign god and savior of children whose bemused, smiling statue everywhere graces cemeteries, roadways, shrines and memorials. Through his eyes, my first weeks in Japan were spent in another century, struggling to understand this new and bewildering environment from the perspective of a lover of *kwaidan* who had searched the world to find his home in what he called "a world where land, life and sky are unlike all that one has known elsewhere."

Unbeknownst to me, the ghost of Lafcadio Hearn had placed himself at my shoulder. Actually, I had not even thought much of him since 1979, when I briefly wore his shoes in a dramatic monologue for an American Studies class on Japanese Americans at the University of Hawaii. I had begun my teaching career with a bizarre taste for the theatrical, donning costumes and make-up so as to present the past through the living words of historical figures.

I had heard about Hearn, as had most students of folklore, through his tales of the supernatural. I had first seen these tales interpreted in the frightening Japanese film, "Kwaidan." The man behind the ghosts, I soon discovered, was as captivating as his *obake* creations. "Becoming" Lafcadio Hearn in words, dress and mannerisms had become my brief obsession.

Not that I really resembled him in any way whatsoever. Indeed, he was something of a gnome-like figure, small in stature and marked by a deformed eye. Neither was his temperament very admirable. Quick tempered, he was known to turn on his best friends, to view the world through an exaggerated love-hate relationship with all things he touched. Even in his beloved Japan, his adopted homeland, he railed against its growing militarism, Westernization and bureaucratic hypocrisy.

Yes, but his words . . . the beauty of his language when he described the crest of a wave along a Japanese coastline, or the power of his haunted tales. Who would ever forget Hoichi the Earless playing his sad dirge for the tragic spirits of the Heike clan, or Yuki-Onna, the Snow Woman, blowing her breath of death upon the poor, freezing woodsman? Beneath the physical and personality deformities, here was a spirit to emulate.

He was born Patrick Lafcadio Hearn on June 27, 1850, on the Ionian island of Santa Maura (Levkas). His parents were Charles Bush Hearn, a British Army surgeon-major, and Rosa Antonia Cassimati Hearn, a dark-haired Greek beauty. They had met while Charles Hearn was stationed in Greece. The wedding of the young British officer and the Greek woman had been opposed by her parents, and the marriage was doomed to unhappiness.

Charles was seldom at home, serving in the Crimean War. Rosa raised Lafcadio and his younger brother at the Dublin, Ireland home of Mrs. Sarah Holmes Brenane, a Hearn relative. Isolated from her family and country, Rosa became distraught and unbalanced, eventually returning to Greece and leaving the care of her children to Mrs. Brenane. Lafcadio would never see his mother again, committing her sacred love to an imperishable memory.

Lafcadio was sent to a Catholic boarding school, where he learned to despise the Church. His misfortunes continued. At the age of 16, his father died while in foreign service, and a playground accident left Lafcadio blind and deformed in his left eye. To compensate for the loss of vision, his right eye became enlarged and overworked, resulting in acute narrow-sightedness. For the rest of his public life, Hearn would instinctively cover his left eye with a raised hand to hide his physical embarrassment.

Behind-the-scenes maneuvering by a cousin named Henry Hearn Molyneux, who sought to inherit the large estate of the elderly Mrs. Brenane, resulted in Hearn being sent to America to live with an uncle in Cincinnati, Ohio in 1869. He was given only $5. When he arrived at his uncle's home, he was informed they had no room, board or money to lend the young European visitor. Penniless, he survived on the streets until finally landing a job at a print shop and later at the Cincinnati Enquirer newspaper.

Mrs. Brenane died in 1871, leaving nothing in her will for

Hearn. He decided to remain in the United States and built a quiet, but distinguished, reputation as a journalist in Cincinnati and then New Orleans. He possessed a flair for poetry and the dramatic, and developed an interest in the sensational, frequently writing about reported ghost sightings, gruesome murders, or other topics pandering to the popular taste.

Slightly Bohemian in dress and lifestyle, he shocked his friends and fellow workers when he married a young mulatto named Mattie Foley. Hearn's taste for women had also been towards the exotic, perhaps lured by the dark-skinned memory of his own Greek mother, whom he sometimes described as a "gypsy." His willingness to defy the laws of miscegenation and fly in the face of mainstream propriety led Hearn to study voodoo and Creole cultures, producing his first major publication in 1887, "Some Chinese Ghosts," which was based on stories collected among Chinese in the United States, and an 1889 romance novelette titled "China."

Then came the assignment that would change his life. In March 1890 an assignment with Harper's Weekly took Hearn to Japan to produce a series of essays on this remarkable Asian nation that had moved from a bastion of feudalism to world power in less than 30 years. When his steamer pulled into Tokyo Bay, Mt. Fuji clearly in the distance, an excited Lafcadio Hearn reportedly said to a companion, "I want to die here." "I want to *live* here," calmly responded his friend.

By the end of his first year in Japan, Hearn had lost all interest in returning to the United States. Fascinated by all aspects of the country—from its folksongs and tales to the ideograms of its written language, to its Buddhist and Shinto gods, to the remote world of its village life—he obtained a good-paying job teaching English in a government school in the village of Matsue on the Sea of Japan.

This was to be his happiest time in Japan, instructing his polite, obedient students, struggling with his never-to-be-fully mastered Japanese language, exploring shrines and the countryside, and finally marrying Setsuko Koizumi, the only daughter of an impoverished samurai family.

Hearn returned to Tokyo to avoid the biting winters of Matsue and taught at the Imperial University and, later, Waseda University. During that time he published numerous works on Japan, interpreting the customs, values, religions, folklore and culture of this once-isolated country for the English-speaking world. Through "Glimpses of Unfamiliar Japan" (1894), "Out of the East" (1895), "Kokoro" (1896), "Gleanings in Buddha-Fields" (1897), "Exotics and the Retrospectives" (1898), "In Ghostly Japan" (1899), "Shadowings" (1900), "A Japanese Miscellany" (1901), "Kotto" (1902), "Kwaidan" (1904), "Japan: An Attempt at Interpretation" (1904), and "The Romance of the Milky Way" (1905), Hearn earned an international reputation.

He was to the Japanese, who received him as the naturalized citizen, Koizumi Yakumo. At the age of 54, Hearn, the father of two young sons and a daughter by his Japanese wife, suffered a heart attack and died at his desk. He is buried at the Zoshigaya Public Cemetery in Tokyo.

As far as obsessions go, "being Lafcadio Hearn" was one of the more short-lived ones in my life. I laid him aside after only one performance, plowing through historic pastures far closer to my Hawaii home. Yet, here I was a decade later, prancing around Japan, occasionally getting lost on the trains, confused by the *kapakahi* streets, telling whomever would listen that I was studying Lafcadio Hearn. Amazingly, I always got a smile of recognition—all generations of Japanese still had knowledge of, if not a fondness for, this peculiar *gaijin*.

One of the individuals to whom I confessed my interest in Hearn was Noriko Nakamura, the assistant who had been assigned to me at the university. Nakamura-san was a recent graduate of the University of the Air and an active volunteer at the school. She was an instructor in traditional Japanese cuisine and a world traveler who dutifully performed her duties as housewife and mother, and who soon became both my right and left hands at the school. In our spare time we visited museums and regional culture centers, explored nearby shrines, and taught each other our respective languages. In a small graveyard at a Shinto shrine outside of Narita, she told me the legend of a *tanuki* (badger) who had died in this shrine and was memorialized in legend. I mentioned my love for ghost stories and, specifically, my fascination for Lafcadio Hearn. Her eyes opened wide.

"Oh, Grant-sensei. My good friend, Kaoru Sekita, works as an archivist at Waseda University where Hearn last taught. They have some of his private papers. I will call her."

A week later we were in the dark tomb of the Waseda archives, Sekita-san spreading out before me the precious documents written by Hearn that the school still retained following his sudden and tragic death. She handled them so gingerly, unlike the white-gloved sanitation I had become accustomed to in archives, it seemed as if his small journal books, personal notes and jottings belonged to someone who was still alive, sitting in a nearby alcove. I held his things in my hands and was stirred by the immediacy of the past.

Outside the archive vault and in the back of the library's foyer, Sekita-san showed us a scroll painting that belonged to the school, but was now hidden behind a protective screen. Years of sunlight had faded the paint so that now only the most curious saw the wonderful portrait of Lafcadio Hearn, sitting upon a *zabuton*, bedecked in kimono with his family *mon*, his beloved Japanese smoking pipes strewn nearby, and a stack of his more famous publications on Japan near at hand.

As Nakamura-san and I left Waseda that dark, drizzly afternoon, our bags stuffed with mementos given to us by Sekita-san, we had made arrangements for all three of us to travel to Matsue in February. We would visit the village which Hearn most loved and pay homage at his home, still standing.

I should make it perfectly clear that I never misrepresented myself as an expert "Hearn scholar" at the University of Hawaii. I had merely said that I was interested in the man, was conducting "research" on his life in Japan, and was myself a collector of ghost stories. Never did I say I had contributed my scholarly essays on his works or biography to any learned journals.

When we finally arrived at the airport in Izumo, I had no expectation of receiving any red carpet treatment from the community of Hearn scholars who lived in the region. Therefore, you can understand my embarrassment when a small delegation met us at the airport, eagerly shaking my hand as one of their counterparts in Hawaii. The most venerable of the representatives of

Hearniana was Professor Yasuyuki Kajitani, emeritus professor of English at an international university in Kyoto, now a resident of Izumo, near "Hearn country."

Knowing it was my first visit to Japan, Kajitani-sensei had carefully prepared xeroxed readings from the writings of Lafcadio Hearn for our tour of the region. We piled into a small chauffeured limousine and sped along an open country road. Sensei slowly read the appropriate selections, recreating the impressions of the man whom he had lovingly studied for over 50 years.

At the sacred Izumo Taisha Shrine, we stood outside a forbidden enclosure as sensei explained how Hearn had been the first *gaijin* to step foot inside this area under the escort of the high priest. The reverence this peculiar foreigner had for Japanese religion and folkways was instantly communicated to those around him, so Hearn would be one of the few outsiders to be truly embraced by the race of Nippon.

From shrine to graveyard, from samurai house to castle, we journeyed through Izumo and nearby Matsue, listening to the measured words of Sensei reading an ageless description, a collected ghost story, or similar passages from the master's work.

In the midst of a new urban development, we visited the tomb of the pregnant mother who had been mistakenly buried before her actual death, giving birth to her son in the coffin. Her ghost had later appeared at a small store, where it obtained a piece of sweet bean cake. When the cries of the newborn infant were heard in the graveyard, the coffin was disinterred, the corpse of the mother clinging to her baby, whose mouth still had upon it the evidence of the bean cake his mother's spirit had retrieved!

Later that afternoon at Mionoseki—where we had seen the ageless ritual of the *mika* dance—we shared a delicious meal of *soba*, with, of course, appropriate quotes from Hearn read by our teacher. Sensei then suddenly laid aside his *hashi*, leaned towards me at the table, and asked directly, "What is your interest in Hearn?"

The simple, but direct, question tied my tongue. He may have expected a scholarly response, but I confessed that my interest was now growing more emotional. "I like to think, Sensei, that I'm a little like Hearn. He came to Japan and discovered the beauty of their soul through their lore. I came to Hawaii and found a similar beauty in their ghost stories. We are both collectors of tales."

"Ah," he muttered. "Yes, I understand. You have been touched by him also. Sekita-san, you must make sure that he meets Koizumi-san. He is a young man, but you will like him very much. He is much like his great-grandfather."

Bon Koizumi lives in Matsue and is the curator of the Lafcadio Hearn Memorial Museum. My first impression was that he was much younger a man than I had expected, but his soft manner and delicate features were not unlike those of his venerated ancestor. Indeed, young Koizumi-san's profile was identical to that of his great-grandfather, with a distinctly shaped nose that revealed his Eurasian heritage. Since his English was extremely limited, we mostly spoke through Nakamura-san.

He escorted us through the old house in which Lafcadio Hearn had spent most of his time while in Matsue, the small garden in which he spent many hours meditating, and the room which was his study. The grand tour of the historic house and museum was made all the more memorable because a descendant had been our guide. My only discomfort throughout the whole journey was that if I had been given this treatment because I was mistakenly believed to be an authority on Hearn, then I was guilty of being an impostor.

"When you return to Tokyo," Koizumi-san said as we made our farewells, "you must attend the ceremony honoring the opening of the Hearn Library in Ireland. It will be a very nice event. The Irish ambassador to Japan will be there. Also, my father."

The formal reception honoring the establishment of the Hearn Library in Dublin, Ireland was in conjunction with the Japanese celebration of the 100th anniversary of Hearn's arrival in Japan. A major conference honoring the writer's Japanese connection was scheduled for August 1990 in Matsue, with scholars traveling from around the world to participate. I was, of course, asked repeatedly if I was attending or delivering any remarks. My answer was always a quietly muttered, "I'm not sure at this time."

It was during the last week of March, just a few days before my scheduled return to Hawaii, that the reception took place at a hotel in downtown Tokyo. Nakamura-san and I arrived to find a harried Sekita-san running about, making sure that everything was going smoothly. Only then did I learn that she was one of the major coordinators of the Hearn anniversary events and had even assembled a small photographic exhibit on the writer's life which had been mounted for the reception.

As hundreds of visitors and dignitaries moved about the hall, she led us through the mob, introducing us in Japanese to this person and that with enough authority in her voice to know that I was being presented as the Hawaii expert on Hearn. I begged Nakamura-san to explain to Sekita-san that I was embarrassed by the hyperbole. She smiled and shrugged at my perceived modesty.

Within 15 minutes, I had met the Irish ambassador and his staff and then Toki Koizumi, the grandson of Lafcadio Hearn. Then Sekita-san whisked me off, elbowing her way through a crowd gathered about an old gentleman standing straight as an arrow and looking a bit overwhelmed by the attention he was receiving. He looked hauntingly familiar. Nakamura-san excitedly tapped my shoulder, whispering, "Grant-sensei, it is the Crown Prince."

I froze. Of course, he looked exactly like his brother, the former Emperor Showa. Sekita-san made the introduction and I could hear her say, "Hearn," "Obake," and "Hawaii." What in the hell was she telling him?

He extended his hand, looked quizzically at me, and uttered only one word in English, "Ghosts?" Chickenskin covered my body as I shook the Crown Prince's hand. My tongue froze, groping for a response.

Before I could answer, a thousand light bulbs exploded and we were all asked to turn around for an official portrait. I knew I had absolutely no right to be standing there, the great Hearn scholar impostor immortalized in photograph! The Irish ambassador standing next to me whispered in my ear, "I think we have just become famous."

I spent the rest of the evening hiding in the men's room, convinced that if the deception continued I was certain to be arrested. At the end of the evening, I regrouped with my two cohorts. Sekita-san asked when my plane left. *"Doyobi,"* I told her.

"Good," she replied. Friday she had made an appointment for me to go to the home of Toki Koizumi for a private meeting.

My six months in Japan had passed far more quickly than I could have ever anticipated. The thought of returning to Hawaii seemed foreboding—as if I was to pick up the yoke of a heavy burden that I had left far behind. Here was a new life and adventure that I had only been given the opportunity to see, not fully experience. As the date of departure approached, I grew more sullen. I absorbed the few sights and sounds left to me of Japan like a man doomed to see them nevermore.

I didn't know what to expect of my visit with Mr. Koizumi. I had seen him only briefly at the reception, but I had been impressed with the similarity of his profile to that of his son. He and his gracious wife lived in the suburbs of Tokyo, and our whirlwind guide, as usual, took us to his doorstep as if we were in a foot race.

Toki Koizumi, who is in his early 70s, answered the door and escorted us into a parlor filled with the bric-a-brac of small figurines that he and his wife had collected in their many world travels. His movements were extremely careful, almost delicate in a manner similar to the *mika* dancer.

His voice trembled slightly when he spoke his measured English, as did his hands as he turned the pages of a family album that had been given to him by his father, Lafcadio Hearn's son, Kazuo Koizumi. The photographs were of the Koizumi family and their famous ancestor, shots of the family home in Tokyo, and of the infant grandson.

I especially remember one photograph taken in 1945. Kazuo Koizumi, now a distinguished old man, stood in the midst of a barren, charred field where the family house had once stood. The house had been destroyed during one of the fire-bombings of Tokyo during the last months of the war. A few belongings of Hearn, one of his smoking pipes and a *hanko* (stamp), were placed delicately in my hand.

Our conversation was not marked by any subterfuge on my part. I spoke frankly and told Mr. Koizumi that I was not a scholar of Hearn's life and work, but a collector of tales who had simply come to greatly admire this man who had the ability to bridge two worlds through the lore and song of a unique race.

"Yes, I understand," he assured me. He then took my hand and led me into a separate room, hidden by *shoji* doors from the parlor. We took off our house slippers as he escorted me before the shrine of his grandfather, the Buddhist *ihai*, or tablet, inscribed upon his death prominently placed before an old, yellowed photograph. Lighting a stick of incense, its pungent odor invoking the timeless presence of spirit, I stiffly bowed and put the offering in the sand before the shrine.

I had watched the religious rituals of Buddhism performed many times, but had never myself felt comfortable enough to be anything but a witness. Yet, before the spirit of Lafcadio Hearn, I clapped twice, softly, hoping to catch the attention of the gods in their eternal abode. My journey to Japan had come to an end, and I wept silently before his ghost.

On the long plane ride home, I read a small passage from Hearn's "The Romance of the Milky Way," whose beautiful melancholy had always haunted me. Written near the end of his life, it expressed the sense of incompleteness he felt in his attempt to touch Old Japan, a world that was fading so quickly from the world scene. It speaks of the loneliness felt by the *gaijin* who reaches out to the world beyond his reach, a world now in my memory, filled with the pleasant company of friends and adventures, haunted by the ghost of Lafcadio Hearn who, perhaps, had turned the many coincidences into purpose.

An old, old sea-wall, stretching between two boundless levels, green and blue; —on the right only rice-fields, reaching to the sky-line; on the left only summer-silent sea, where fishing-craft of curious shapes are riding. Everything is steeped in white sun; and I am standing on the wall. Along its broad and grass-grown top a boy is running towards me, —running in sandals of wood, —the sea-breeze blowing aside the long sleeves of his robe as he runs, and baring his slender legs to the knee. Very fast he runs, springing upon his sandals; —and he has in his hands something to show me: a black dragonfly, which he is holding carefully by the wings, lest it should hurt itself struggling . . . With what sudden incommunicable pang do I watch the gracious little figure leaping in the light, —between those summer silences of field and seal . . . A delicate boy, with the blended charm of two races . . . And how softly vivid all things under this milky radiance, —the smiling child-face with lips apart, —the twinkle of the light quick feet, —the shadows of grasses and of little stones! . . .

"But, quickly as he runs, the child will come no nearer to me, —the slim brown hand will never cling to mine. For this light is the light of a Japanese sun that set long years ago . . . Never, dearest! —never shall we meet, —not even when the stars are dead!

"And yet, —can it be possible that I shall not remember? — that I shall not still see, in other million summers, the same sea-wall under the same white noon, —the same shadows of grasses and of little stones, —the running of the same little sandalled feet that will never, never reach my side?"

Farewell, Lafcadio Hearn. May your spirit find its solace finally in the soul of your adopted land.

The Kasha Of Kaimuki

Arthur McDougal, a retired Honolulu International Detective Agency operative who took the Big Sleep a few years ago in a North Shore sanitarium, had spent the majority of his life pursuing flesh-and-blood kidnappers, murderers, embezzlers, adulterers and sundry felons, risking his life and keeping the streets of Honolulu clean for only twenty-five dollars a day. Many of his misadventures in crime detection were told to me before his death and will hopefully appear one day in print as The McDougal Files. Undoubtedly, the most bizarre of his cases he called, simply, "The Kasha of Kaimuki."

In August of 1942 two Honolulu police officers were called to a home in Kaimuki, somewhere near Harding Avenue. The dispatcher had told the officers that there was some kind of domestic disturbance taking place. As they pulled up in front of the house, a woman was wildly screaming, "She's trying to kill my children! She's trying to kill my children!" as she sprinkled salt from a ti leaf about the yard. "What's going on?" the officers asked, and the hysterical woman could only point to the house and mutter again and again, "She's killing my children!"

Rushing the front door, the officers stumbled onto a scene that they would never forget. The three children who lived in the house were flying about the room, levitated, slapped and hurled by an invisible force. Unable to enter the room or quell the inexplicable disturbance, the officers watched for an hour-and-a-half as the children were assaulted by an unseen and unknown entity. "My mother-in-law hated me," later explained the mother of the victimized children. "Now that she is dead, she is an evil spirit who is trying to hurt my children." The story was briefly reported in the Honolulu Star-Bulletin. The officers would not give an interview concerning the terror that they had seen.

Thirty years later, another incident took place in a house near Harding Avenue. A young girl had been assaulted by another "unseen force." Fleeing her house, she and her boyfriend drove off and got as far as the parking lot of a popular nightspot at the junction of Waialae and Kapiolani boulevards. The police called to the scene reported that a girl was being beaten in the back seat of an automobile by an unseen force. As they entered the car to help her, they were both thrown back to the ground. This incident lasted fifteen minutes and was filed with the HPD under the category of "miscellaneous crime." "A young woman and two officers assaulted by persons unknown." This story also appeared in the local dailies.

What force could hurl persons through the air, levitating them for an hour-and-a-half? Why did two such occurrences take place so close to each other on Harding Avenue? What unleashed demon waits to rip your flesh apart, tearing living and dead asunder? If you believe in such things, perhaps it is a kasha, the Japanese specter who bears bodies away, to break them into pieces and consume their flesh.

McDougal, private operative for nearly thirty-five years with the Honolulu International Detective Agency, told me on several occasions that he was one haole who never believed in ghosts. Yet there was one murder case, he admitted to me before his death, that he could never forget. "Hell, I don't think it was a spook," he shot at me from his sanitarium bed, "but, kid, it was something not of this world." And it all started in a house on Harding Avenue somewhere in Kaimuki . . .

The rain came down like bullets, pelting the roof of my old Plymouth that chugged along down Kapahulu Avenue, spitting exhaust and giving a bath to the few fool pedestrians who were standing too close to the flooded curbs. This town wasn't made for heavy rains, I muttered as my sedan swerved around a pothole, taking a heavy dose of blood-red Kaimuki mud across my front grill.

"May Kats Oyama rot in hell," I swore to no one in particular. "The next time that kid needs help, he can call some other private dick."

I didn't really mean it. Kats Oyama was the son of the best partner a gumshoe could have ever had—Shige Oyama, a slick-dressing, smooth-talker from Yokohama who had come to Hawaii to make his fortune in the sugar fields and ended up walking a beat in Tin Can Alley. While Chang "Charlie Chan" Apana was busy playing mahjong and spilling his guts to Earl Biggers, Shige was out busting heads in "Little Tokyo." He came up against some of the toughest hombres you'd ever want to meet who called themselves the Hinode or "Rising Sun" gang. These Japanese hoods ran all the brothels, hootch parlors and cocaine trade down on Pauahi Street and had gotten so bold they even printed their own newspaper. It took a gutsy guy like Shige to infiltrate their ranks and break up their rackets, sending most of them on to L.A. or Frisco. After he quit the H.P.D. to become an operative for the Honolulu International Detective Agency, we often worked on the same cases, tracking down some adulterous husband or putting a tail on a suspected embezzler. Then there was that night in a Pawaa Japanese theater when Shige took a .38 slug just below his right ear. It was lights out for Oyama.

It isn't right when your partner dies and all the witnesses have amnesia. So, you file the case in the back of your mind as "open," and you feel a little sorry for the kid who wants to be a gumshoe like his dad so that maybe one day he can nail the s.o.b. who made him an orphan. Kats Oyama was so green, you could plant a good-sized bonsai tree behind his ears. But when he actually got his first case, he was so thrilled I couldn't help but agree to give him some fatherly advice. After all, it seemed a pretty routine investigation.

A family by the name of Uemoto had hired Kats to check out the background of their son's fiancee. Seemed he had fallen head over heels for a sweet dish from Tokyo who claimed to be the daughter of a baron and spoke Danish like a pro. For nearly ten years she had gone to boarding school in Copenhagen, where her legs grew out long and shapely and she acquired the name "Aase" Tsutsui. Her curves may not have matched an hourglass, but you could really kill time looking at them.

Shingo Uemoto was a good-looking boy who had broken a couple of the University of Hawaii swimming records before graduating and moving into his father's downtown export business. He and Aase had met at the university, where she was majoring in history—one of those useless subjects I figured only coddled rich kids majored in while they soaked their parents for a living allowance. The way I saw it, Shingo was pretty lucky snaring what had to be the best catch on campus. Only thing was, his parents didn't trust the Danish accent coming out of a great pair of Japanese lips. They wanted Kats to dig something up on her—like maybe her father was a yakuza, or her grandaunt was "kichigai."

I had wired our Tokyo offices for Kats and put the international boys on her tail. So far, they hadn't turned up anything we hadn't already known. Of course, with all the war talk that summer and F.D.R. having frozen Japanese assets in the U.S. last June, getting any government agency in Japan to turn any information over to foreign private investigators was nearly impossible. In fact, the Chief had already decided to pull our men back to Hawaii, just in case all the hot air between Tokyo and Washington turned lethal.

I had been meaning to tell Kats that Aase Tsutsui had come out with a clean bill of health, when my secretary China tracked me down that night at the Waikiki Tavern, where I was drinking a few Schofield doughfaces under the table. She told me that a frantic Kats had called the office from the Uemoto home in Kaimuki. He asked that I hustle over, mumbling something about "bigger than I thought." So, while I should of been dry and cozy at a bar in Waikiki, I was driving through the muck and mire of Kaimuki on a stormy October night, trying to be a good Samaritan to an amateur dick. If I had had any sense in my head, I would have remembered that charity and detective work don't mix.

The Plymouth plowed through one more mudbath before I turned onto Harding. China told me to look for a two-story white house sitting on a foundation of huge lava boulders near the corner of Eighth and Harding. It was one of those pretty Kaimuki houses that had been built back in the twenties, when all the Portuguese, Chinese and Japanese who could afford it were eager to buy up homes in the new suburbs. It was a decent little neighborhood of hard-working families, mama and papasan stores, a Japanese language school, saimin stands, and even a miniature golf course. It was the kind of cozy place where you raised your kids, paid your taxes and, like every other American in 1941, buried your head in the sand. It was the last place you would have ever expected a murder.

The "Honolulu Poi Dogs," or H.P.D., had already arrived on the scene by the time I pulled up in front of the house. They were busy roping off the yard and keeping the curious, rain-drenched neighbors from peeking in the windows. When Chief of Detectives Johnny MacIntosh saw me, he waved me past the barricade and shuffled me onto the lanai, where two cops in a state of shock were trying to give their statements. They were making about as much sense as a pair of baboons at the Honolulu Zoo.

"What gives, Johnny?"

"I was about to ask you the same thing, Mac. Funny seeing you here. You got business inside?"

"Maybe, maybe not," I answered. With MacIntosh I could afford to be a little coy. After all, I had taught him everything he knew about police work before he replaced me as Chief of Detectives. "All right, I was called by Kats Oyama to meet him here. What's goin' on?"

"Damndest thing. An hour ago dispatch received a call from the neighbors that there were shrieks coming from this house and that a woman was hysterical in the yard. Those two pale-faced officers showed up and tried to get in the house, but, according to them, they couldn't get in."

"Why didn't they just kick in the door."

"You don't understand, Mac. They told us they couldn't get in. The door was wide open, only something they couldn't see

105

kept them out."

"You better check their breath, Johnny."

"The old woman, Mrs. Uemoto, she verifies it. Something was in the house, they say, that was smashing furniture and attacking anyone who tried to come in. It seemed to be after her son who, according to the officers, was floating smack-dab in the middle of the room while all the fracas was going on. Her husband was pretty seriously hurt. He suffered a concussion when he was thrown to the ceiling. I'm afraid Kats was also banged up pretty bad. They've already hauled him off to emergency. And get this part, Mac. The officers say that the attack lasted nearly an hour!"

"And they never saw anything?"

"Nothing. But they felt it. The blows felt like sledge hammers to their chest."

"What about the son, Shingo?"

"Dead. What's left of him is scattered on the walls."

Johnny warned me that it wasn't going to be a pretty sight . . . and that was an understatement. The blood-soaked interior of the room and all the furniture had been smashed to a million bits—as if a tornado had torn into Kaimuki. The only time I had seen this kind of carnage was in the Great War, when boys were blown to pieces by German fire. Only at least a cannonball is mercifully swift. Shingo Uemoto had been methodically pulled apart by the arms, legs and head before his torso was ripped in half like a gutted fish. The pattern of bloodstains on the wall and floor suggested that he had been evidently spun in mid-air until he literally exploded. The dismembering could have been done with the powerful blows of a sword, but the circular profusion of blood suggested a centrifugal force, as if the boy had been hit by an airplane propeller. If it hadn't of been so damned curious, I would have puked my guts up.

"So what do you think, Mac?" Johnny asked from the outside. He had glanced at the scene of the murder only once and was letting us with stronger stomachs sort through the human rubble.

"I can't buy the supernatural twist. Maybe hallucination, or hypnotism. But poltergeists? I've been in this business long enough to know that a dead body usually means that somebody on this side of the veil was mighty anxious to make sure that somebody else crossed over to the other side."

"Kasha," a frail, frightened voice added from a corner darkness. She had been standing there, unnoticed, since I first had entered the room, silently watching over the sundered remains of what had once been her only son. Dressed in a simple, dark-gray house dress, her jet-black hair pulled back into a matronly bun, Mrs. Uemoto typified what us haoles in Hawaii had learned to recognize as that horde of older issei ladies who hardly ever spoke English, always avoided looking you in the eye, and could always be found lining up for the Saturday matinee at the Toyo Theater on College Walk. You usually dismissed them as part of the Hawaiian landscape, but this one had an eerie look of despair and hatred that riveted me to the spot.

"Kasha," she murmured again and then fell silent.

"What do you mean?"

"She doesn't speak English," MacIntosh chimed in. "That's all she's said since we got here. I let one of our Japanese men try to talk to her but we can't get anything more than that one word. He's calling a doctor friend right now that speaks her lingo. She won't let no one touch her. Mental breakdown, I guess."

"What does it mean, kasha?"

"Got me. The officer who talked to her is a nisei. Says it's a word he doesn't know. Must be from the old country. By the way, what were you and Kats working on, McDougal? Why would the Uemotos need a detective?"

"Just a couple of background checks for the family business," I vaguely lied. "Nothing really too important. If you don't mind, I'll leave you to this mess and look in on Kats."

I was walking back to my Plymouth through the throngs of neighbors and reporters, who had already started the Honolulu rumor mill rolling when MacIntosh called after me.

"Mac, honestly, what do you make of it?"

"If your officers saw and experienced what they said they did, then I'd say you need an exorcist on this case, not cops."

"Should we get ourselves blessed?" he asked me with the sincerity of someone who may have never seen a ghost, but has lived long enough in the Islands to develop an open mind.

"Go ahead, it won't hurt. As for me, I'm going to bless myself with a bottle of Five Island gin." And, after calling the hospital to make sure that Kats was sleeping sound and safe, that's exactly what I did before falling into a peaceful sleep that was disturbed only twice by a dream of screaming banshee.

The next two days were spent shuttling between Emergency Hospital with magazines and candies for Kats and prying into the Bethel station to get any news MacIntosh was willing to spill on Shingo Uemoto's death. By now the story told by the two officers had become the talk of Honolulu. Everybody and their cousin had a theory about how bodies could be levitated and a human being literally blown apart. My Chinese barber at the Alexander Young Hotel tried to convince me it was the work of vampires from China who consumed human flesh. I needed to remind him that nothing had been eaten.

Quite honestly, it was none of my business what happened in that Kaimuki house. It was Kats' contract, not mine. With a few broken ribs and some internal bleeding, the kid wasn't going to be leaving Emergency at least for a couple of weeks and he begged me to look into it.

"Mac," he said, with that plaintive look he always used so well, "if my reputation is going to remain unsullied, then I can't just let my clients get killed and do nothing. Geez, this is my first case! Just look into it until I'm back on my feet."

"Well, if I stick my nose in this nonsense, I want to know why in the hell you called me that night. China told me you told her it was 'bigger than you had thought.' What did you mean by that?"

"While you were helping me out with the Tokyo connection on Miss Tsutsui, I had been nosing around at the University of Hawaii, just trying to find out what kind of student she was. It didn't take long for me to find out that she was dating a lot more men than Shingo. In fact, I guess you could say she had pretty hot pants. I counted at least three other students who claimed that they had nailed her . . . and Mac, if you can believe it, she's even sleeping around with a professor. They spent a weekend at the Crouching Lion together when his wife was visiting Hilo.

Even though Mrs. Uemoto was the one who was paying my fee, I figured I'd tell Shingo first. We used to play baseball together at Moiliili field when we were kids—so, shucks, I at least owed him that. I mean, that would have been real shame to let his mother know first. Japanese families can get really worked up over stuff like this, you know, Mac?

"So did you tell him," I asked.

"Yeah, but he never acted mad or anything. It was like he knew. He said that there was something else he found out and that he needed my help. He thought I was too young to handle it so he asked me to call you up and have you come over to his house that night. I show up and the next thing you know, the world turns crazy. You don't know what it's like, Mac, to be lifted off your feet, spun around like a top and then dropped like a rag doll."

"Don't be so sure," I answered, remembering a great weekend in Tijuana. "There's one more thing, Kats, do you know what kasha means? Mrs. Uemoto was muttering it that night."

"Hell, Mac, I don't speak Japanese," he said, with a big grin that reminded me of his dad and an unfulfilled obligation. I assured him that I would help him out the best I could, but, when he got on his own two feet, this was one nightmare of a case he could tackle himself.

In the matter of a murdered man whose fiancee is sleeping with half of the University of Hawaii faculty, it seems reasonable to begin the investigation with the object of desire. It wasn't difficult to find Aase Tsutsui or the Nuuanu house her family rented for her on Wyllie Street. First off, Kats had the address and, secondly, it was the biggest estate in that old historic section of town next to the Oahu Cemetery.

A Filipino house servant in a crisply ironed white uniform answered the door. When I asked for Miss Tsutsui, he ushered me to a side room while he called the "ma'am." For a student attending the University of Hawaii, I thought, this spread was one hell of a dormitory. The entryway was adorned with fancy European vases and paintings that belonged more in a museum than a home. My plebeian tastes preferred my dingy Waikiki cottage to all this palatial crap, but it would of spun the head of a boy like Shingo Uemoto.

I was wondering what would have attracted Aase Tsutsui to a simple Kaimuki boy when she stepped into the room. What would attract her to a pudgy, middle-aged Honolulu detective who's getting gray at the temples and cold in the heart, I then thought. I guess at that moment I would have sold my soul to the devil for the answer. If she was wearing a stylized ebony-black dress out of respect for the dead, it should have covered more of her long legs and cleavage. Her intriguing, almond eyes were encased in the loveliest face that had ever been crafted from an Asian mold. Despite her womanly beauty, I couldn't help but notice that the slight pout of her lips and the way her long, black hair fell across her shoulders seemed almost childish.

She introduced herself to me, speaking perfect English with a tinge of Danish accent, acknowledging my professional interest in the death of her fiance and assuring me that she had told the police all that she could about the horrible incident. As she spoke, I gazed at the slight curve of her long neck and saw us gently floating in a Sumida River sampan past the rows of sakura blooming and a Danish windmill turning in the wind as we brought our lips . . .

"Mister McDougal, are you listening to me? Are you all right? I was saying that I told the police everything I know."

"Excuse me," I gingerly lied, "the humidity is stifling after all the rain we've had. Well, I don't want to detain you, Miss Tsutsui, but is there anyone who you can think of who would want Shingo dead?"

"You think someone murdered him? I thought that it was . . . supernatural?"

"Do you believe that?"

"Well, the circumstances seem most bizarre. . ."

"Hallucinations, hypnotism, there may be plenty of explanations for the bizarre. But your fiance is dead, and anything you can tell me would help."

"She killed him! First she stole him from me and then she killed him!"

The voice came from behind me and I turned to see a round-faced young woman in a yellow summer dress whose eyes were livid in rage.

"I loved Shingo. How do you think she meet him? I introduced them. She kills everything she touches."

Aase rattled off something in Japanese and, just as suddenly and as violently as she had appeared, the apparition vanished into a back room.

"Tomoko is my younger sister. When my mother died, our father, who is Baron Tsutsui, separated us. She came to Hawaii and attended Mid-Pacific School. I was sent to Copenhagen for my education. We hadn't seen each other in years, when my father asked that I come to the Islands to care for my sister. You see, doctors have diagnosed her as suffering from acute schizophrenia. She claims not only to see spirits, but believes that I have destroyed her life. Actually, Shingo and I met quite without introductions from Tomoko. It was love at first sight, as the Americans call it. I know of no one who would have hurt him. He may have been a simple man, but he was extraordinarily kind, Mr. McDougal. Now, if you'll excuse me, I must tend to my sister."

"If you don't mind, I have only one more question," I added before she slipped out back to the Japanese gardens, which had been landscaped around a small teahouse. The strange little drama between her and her sister hadn't ruffled any of her beautiful feathers, but talking about Shingo had made her eyes glassy, so she carefully daubed the tears without smearing the perfect mascara. "Do you know a professor of history at the University named Arnold Cummins?"

"Dr. Cummins? Yes. I took a history course from him last semester. What would that have to do with Shingo's death?" A flash of concern and anger clearly registered in those exotic eyes.

"Nothing," I assured her, as I turned into the front hall and was nearly bulldozed over by a stout, shaved-head gentleman with a glare so stern that it reminded me of an English teacher every kid has had once in his life. He was carrying a small medical bag and was sputtering something in Japanese that sailed right past me. Something had made him hopping mad and he sure in the hell was letting Aase know. When he finished scolding her, he made a beeline for the room where Aase's younger sister had concealed herself. With a brusque knock, he rapped upon the door once and then entered, disappearing as fast as he had appeared.

Trailing not four feet behind the surly little man was a far more calm specimen of humanity who, when she came into the vestibule, bowed very low. Her manner was so calm and controlled, so much unlike the man she followed, that it seemed they made a perfect yin-yang partnership. The silk kimono she was wearing was so tastefully styled and deliciously odorous that it added a certain sophistication to her demeanor. Sweet incense smell—like that burned at an altar—seemed to float about her like an aura. Like many Japanese women, she too seemed to be impervious to aging, although I guessed she must have been in her middle sixties.

"Excuse me, Mr. McDougal. This is Mrs. Mori, my neighbor. The gentleman was her husband, who is also my sister's private physician. Tomoko must have evidently called Dr. Mori following her outburst."

Mrs. Mori bowed once more and then, speaking something in Japanese to Aase, joined her husband in Tomoko's room.

"You'll excuse me, Mr. McDougal," I heard the bum's rush coming on, "I have many things to attend to."

"The funeral?"

"No, my sister and I are going back to Japan just as soon as we can settle matters here. With the world on the brink of war and Nazis tramping all over Europe and my country under the terror of militarism, I really don't know what to do. Shingo and I were going to run away, but now where can I go except home?"

When she burst out crying and quickly rushed out of the room, I couldn't figure out whether I had just seen a woman on the verge of a nervous breakdown or a very fine actress. Either way, I figured my little visit had spoiled enough of her day, so I quietly let myself out and walked back to my machine at curbside. I figured it wouldn't hurt to pick up a little history lesson from Dr. Cummins on fraternizing with Eurasian students.

The campus of the University of Hawaii was alive that month with all kinds of political rallies to discuss the international tensions between Japan and the United States. The isolationists were always singing the praises of Charles Lindbergh, who had snuggled up a little too close to Hitler for my liking, while the interventionists liked to kiss the hand of Stalin, another fellow who looked more like a felon than a politician, if there was a difference. I found Cummins in a small cubicle office in the basement of Hawaii Hall, where he was hiding behind a stack of volumes on European history. I had expected an older man, associating most professors with cobwebbed old codgers. In fact, he wasn't much older than his students, which explained the attraction to Aase. He struck me as one of those haole mainlanders who come over here to teach at the college and fall hard for oriental women. They usually ended up divorcing their poor wife whose only crime was being born white and boring. I figured the best approach wasn't to play cat and mouse, but to use intimidation.

It worked. Within five minutes he not only confessed to an affair with Aase Tsutsui, but with two other students. I think he looked upon me as his confessor priest.

"You can't imagine, Mr. McDougal, what it is like when a woman like that sits in class everyday, looking up to you as if you are a god. When she invited me to the Halekulani Hotel for Sunday brunch, how could I have refused? One thing led to another and I guess you know the rest. You don't think I had something to do with that boy's awful death, the one she was engaged to? I may have loved Aase, but I knew she was only using me to meet other professors on campus. She is insatiable. Yes, quite simply insatiable."

"What's your specialty, Cummins?"

"Medieval Europe. What does that . . ."

"Funny kind of book for a medieval scholar to be reading, isn't it?"

I had picked up off his desk a copy of a pamphlet entitled Pule Anaana: The Art of Hawaiian Sorcery. With all the hocus-pocus talk of the last few days, I thought it was kind of a funny coincidence that a man who obviously had fallen in love with this femme fatale, whose fiance was torn asunder by some unseen force, should be reading a book on sorcery.

"My interest is supernatural lore and medieval witchcraft. While I concentrate on European studies, since I'm living in

Hawaii, I've become interested in Polynesian belief. Why? Has it become illegal to expand one's knowledge of the world?"

"No. I'm just wondering if you believe in it?"

"Who am I to deny its existence? Witchcraft or demonology is one of the oldest cultural forms of folk belief to have survived to modern times. Look how many people read their horoscopes or seek out their futures through fortunetellers. The popularity of Edgar Cayce illustrates the persistence of magic in our lives. While naysayers discard such psychic phenomenon, some people recognize its potent and even dangerous power. Did you know, Mr. McDougal, that at this very moment the Nazis are studying demonology, both for its supernatural possibilities as well as political benefits? There's more to heaven and hell, Mr. McDougal, than your philosophy could explain."

"By the way, professor, have you ever heard of kasha?"

"Yes, most definitely. In Asia, it is believed that corpses are sometimes stolen by flesh-eaters, vampires if you will, who devour the body and sometimes even snatch the coffin. In Japan, these specters are called kasha, and they exert a tremendous force of evil that has been known to smash houses, lift human beings into the air, and tear bodies into pieces."

"Do they really exist? Is there any evidence?"

"Again with the doubts, Mr. McDougal? Superstitious nonsense of primitive people? Is this somehow connected with the death of the Uemoto boy?"

I had had enough of his smart-aleck tongue and I was about ready to turn our intellectual exchange into a broken nose when his office door flew open and a saucy brunette in a tennis costume bounced in uninvited, plunked her racket on the table, knocking over half a century of history tomes, and chirped up, "How about a plunge in the swimming tank, Doc?"

"Really, Helen. Not in the middle of the day. You don't know who'll be in here?"

"You mean one of your little cuties? Excuse me, mister, are you a student of my husband's."

"No, Mr. McDougal is a private investigator who just happens to be on his way out."

"Oh, have I got an earful for you, mister private dick." She had been hitting the bottle pretty hard that morning and the Jack Daniels reeked from her pores as if she had used it for perfume. I could tell the doc was real nervous that his wife was about to embarrass him, but she was out of control. From the look of things, she had been out of control for a long time.

"I've got a class now. You'll excuse me, Mr. McDougal. If you wish, you may borrow one of my books on Asian demonology. You may find it informative. Helen, why don't you come along with me and let the gentleman do his business?"

She broke away from him and turned towards me with a slight sway in her posture and half-opened eyes.

"This is my business."

Dr. Cummins slammed the door behind him, leaving me with an angry wife who had been neither as dumb nor as passive as her husband had supposed. Sure, she knew all about Aase Tsutsui. In fact, she had been so jealous, she used to do a little detective work herself. She knew, for example, that not only had Aase been having an affair with her husband while engaged to Shingo, but also with some handsome-looking Japanese fellow that she drove out to Aiea with at least once a week. They often went to an old Japanese teahouse on Halawa Heights, where they sipped sake on lonely afternoons, holding hands affectionately, and gazing at the sunsets like long-lost lovers reunited. She had told her husband about Aase's promiscuity, but he didn't seem to mind. So, she sent Shingo an anonymous note hoping that it would destroy their engagement.

"What exactly did you tell him?"

"That the woman he loved was having an affair with my husband and another man, not to mention more if we looked hard enough. She's a tramp. I told him everything."

If all this was supposed to add up to whodunit, how they dunit and why, I sure didn't have a clue. When I got back to my office—rolling over and over in my head the gorgeous Danish-speaking broad, the schizophrenic sister, the pushy physician, the arrogant, adulterous professor, the scorned, drunken wife, and the mysterious Japanese lover—I kept coming back to that blood-stained room in Kaimuki and the severed head of Shingo Uemoto looking up at me with his eyes frozen in horror, while his stunned mother whispered in my ear, "kasha."

China immediately filled me in that the Tokyo office dug something up for me that may be interesting. It seems that, according to Aase and her transcripts at the University, she is about nineteen years old. Her birth certificate in Japan, however, indicates that her age is twenty-six. Why would she lie about her age? Vanity? or Deceit?

I then called Kats to see whether or not he had gotten any information from Shingo before he died indicating that he had received an anonymous letter concerning Aase's infidelity. No, only that he had found something out that was "too big." Did Kats know that Aase was twenty-six, not nineteen? No, he'd of never believed it, she looked so young. Why do you suppose she would have lied?

"Well, when she came to Hawaii last year, Shingo and Tomoko, her sister, had been seeing a lot of each other. Maybe she wanted to make herself seem more attractive to steal Shingo away."

"She told me that Tomoko was mentally ill, that she had never been with Shingo."

"That's a lie, Mac. Shingo told me about Tomoko himself."

If I wanted to get a breakthrough on this case, I reckoned that Miss Tomoko was my lucky lottery number. It must have been only eight-thirty in the evening when I pulled up in front of their Wyllie Street house, but the place seemed sealed up tighter than a drum. The house was completely dark and the garage was empty. Next door, the lights at the Moris' house were blazing, and I could hear a slight bell ringing somewhere inside. It must be dinner time for Dr. Mori. A thorny bush separated the two properties and I scratched myself up something awful climbing into the back garden. I checked a few rear windows, but they were all locked up. They were hiding something in that house, and I figured it was Tomoko.

At first I heard the sound as a low, guttural moan, but it soon grew more enriched, as if someone was chanting. The plaintive wail distinctly came from a small, single-room teahouse in the miniature garden that in the evening moonlight seemed almost ethereal. Through the paper walls, a luminous, yellow glow flickered, calling the moth irresistibly to its consuming fire. Instinct told me that what I'd find within didn't want to be found, so I quietly pulled out my Colt .45 from my shoulder holster, resting the butt comfortably in my right hand, fingering the cold metal of the trigger. When I finally reached the entrance, the monotonous chant within was a wildly eerie sutra that either called up the beasts from hell or the wrath of God from above. With my left hand, I quickly pulled back the shoji door while lunging my body into the room, pistol drawn. A young woman was crouched on the floor praying before some strange-looking altar, her body completely naked except for what looked like tattoo patterns drawn like oriental characters all over her. Her maddening prayer continued even as my rushing body rattled the fragile room.

"Aase?"

"You stupid fool," she screamed, breaking her chant and flinging herself around. Looking me in the face I could see Tomoko's eyes filled with the same horror that had been frozen in the eyes of Shingo's corpse.

"You've destroyed the spell. The kasha comes."

"Listen, sister, you and me need to talk."

It grabbed me literally by the seat of the pants and flung me up towards the ceiling. When I hit the ground, I rolled and let off two slugs into the thing that now moved in the room with us. It was like a black shapeless fog that swirled in on itself, sucking me and everything else into the vortex of its violent grip. I was thrown back over Tomoko, tumbling into the altar and candles that scattered across the tatami floor. She reached out to me— her last desperate act, as her body tore at the seams like an unraveling rag doll. I was staring into her face when her head exploded, the impact of flesh, blood and brains flinging me back into the paper-thin walls that could not hold my weight, catapulting me back into the dark waters of the garden pond.

The black fog swirled towards me as a pungent, yet familiar, smell swept momentarily past, and then a shapely carp wearing a slinky red gown kissed me sweetly on the lips. I dove after her, falling head over heels through an eternity of murky, blood-red waters.

When I came to my senses, the carp in the tight red dress

was nibbling on my ear, proposing marriage as I lay in the shallow waters of a pond, nursing a lump on the back of my head the size of a mango. By the look of things, I had taken out nearly the entire wall of the teahouse when I tumbled back through it following the explosion of Tomoko's body. Sheets of ripped rice paper stained with splattered blood flooded about me as the yellow flames of the burning teahouse danced upon the surface of the pond. By the time I got onto my feet, the structure had become an enormous bon fire, with a torrent of swirling red sparks fleeing into the Nuuanu night like a swarm of fireflies. The valley walls were soon echoing the ugly wail of sirens. Evidently, the upturned altar candles had set the place aflame and whatever remained of poor Tomoko Tsutsui was cremated in the inferno.

When Chief of Detectives MacIntosh found me, I was drying my pond-soaked clothing over an exclusive piece of Copenhagen furniture and helping myself to a swill of Jack Daniels I stole from the Tsutsui liquor cabinet. If it had been any other cop, he would've never believed my story. But MacIntosh had seen the remains of Shingo Uemoto, had heard the eyewitness accounts of the two poi dogs on the scene, and had had himself blessed—twice. Nothing was left of Tomoko Tsutsui to verify what I had seen, but we both knew that I was the last man on earth to believe in ghosts. Or body-crunching kasha.

"What do you make of the tattoos on her body?" he asked me.

"My guess is that it was some kind of protection. I must have interrupted a ceremony to keep the damn thing away. That look in her eye, that look of out-of-control terror, was the same one as on the face of Shingo."

"Well, you can't blame yourself, Mac. After all, what do us haoles know about this kind of stuff? Hell, I still don't know if I believe it."

I knew one haole who knew about this hocus-pocus crap. While MacIntosh staked out the Tsutsui estate waiting for a vanished Aase and firemen poked through the ashes extinguishing the last embers, I paid a midnight call on the Kahala home of Professor Cummins. He and his wife were making out like a couple of dogs and cats in heat, only without none of the lovemaking. I had seen this type of couple a dozen times be-fore—they hate each other's guts so much, they can't bear to be away from each other any longer than necessary before the next fight. So they read about praying people to death or send nasty notes to boyfriends, but they never get the nerve to commit mur-der. Hell, they'll never even have the backbone to get a divorce.

After I interrupted their little tete-a-tete over some new floozy that he had recently made eyes at, I asked the Professor about the tattoos on Tomoko and the ceremony that she seemed to be per-forming in front of the shrine. He was more than cooperative, using my visit as an excuse to escape from his domestic squabbles. Drawing a few doodles on a sheet of paper, he handed it to me with the nauseating paternalism you expect from a teacher.

"Did the 'doodles,' as you describe them, resemble these mark-ings?"

"Yeah. So if they isn't 'doodles,' what are they?" I asked in my most ungrammatical English.

"They are ideographs, Mr. McDougal, what the Japanese call kanji. It is their system of writing imported to Japan from China."

"Why would she have them written all over her body?"

"For protection. You see, someone had written them on her so that an evil spirit would stay away. They must have been a Buddhist sutra, or prayer. The prayers she was reciting when you interrupted her were probably also for protection. To keep the kasha away requires the purification of the body and soul through the citing of the ancient sutra. No doubt you must have also no-ticed the senko?"

"What?"

"Incense. It is sometimes burned to protect the living from the demonic forces of the other world. With the sutra written on her body, the prayers chanted and incense burning, Tomoko was anticipating its arrival. Someone must have been sending it out against her, just as it was sent against the Uemoto boy."

"Thanks, Professor," I suddenly interrupted, recalling a cer-tain familiar sweet odor that had filled the teahouse just before Tomoko's death. Mrs. Mori had been reeking of the same pun-gent smell earlier that day when I had been briefly introduced to her by Aase. Somebody had had to help paint the sutra on

Tomoko's back and, if my guess was right, the demur, sweet woman next door was my leading suspect.

The Professor was, of course, hesitant to let me leave, since Mrs. Cummins had swilled down a couple of more shots of booze and was working up a mighty heady steam of evil spirit. For spiritual advice, I suggested he burn a few sticks of incense and in the future keep his pants zipper locked, especially around his students.

By the time I started out for the Mori house back in Nuuanu, it was approaching the Hour of the Ox, two o'clock in the morning. China, my secretary, always warned me that this was the time when spirits of the dead would appear. After what I had been through that evening, I didn't frankly give a damn. I wanted some answers fast and I would have looked right in the face of the kasha itself to get them. And I almost got the chance.

It hit the side of my Plymouth just as I got to Waialae Avenue and Kapiolani Boulevard, crunching the front left fender so hard that I nearly went into a tailspin. My car skidded into the parking lot of the Hula Rhumba nightclub. The shattered glass of my front windshield sprayed me with a stinging velocity that would have lacerated my face if I hadn't of instinctively thrown up my arms for protection. It boxed me hard across the head as my Plymouth plunged into a concrete wall, setting off a blaring horn and erupting the radiator with a hot steam geyser.

I was never much of a pugilist, preferring pistols to knuckles. Sparring with a few rowdies, however, was nothing compared with boxing something you can't see. You take a few wild jabs at thin air and then realize that the best you can do is just go into a fetal position and pray that you wake up from the nightmare. I can't remember how many blows my head and back took or how often I hit the roof of the car. After about ten minutes, it weakened and then finally vanished.

The taxi driver who drove me home said I looked like a walking dead man and offered to drop me off at Queen's Hospital free of charge. I preferred my own bed with its dirty sheets to a bunch of doctors poking stuff at me. I slept in late the next morning, still feeling the bruises that a hot shower couldn't wash away. The only reason I was still alive, I figured, was because last night was only a warning. The sooner I talked with Mrs. Mori, the longer I was going to stay alive.

Kats' car was a souped-up little Ford roadster that roared up in front of the Mori home and gave a loud cough when I turned off the ignition. Mrs. Mori answered the door, gave one look at my bruised face, and ushered me into a back room, where the smell of burning incense was like a dense San Francisco fog. She tapped a small golden bell several times and began praying in a wondrous sing-song chant that was hypnotic as she held her hands above my head. A glow of heat seemed to penetrate me and, if I hadn't of known better, I would have admitted that I felt like a million dollars.

An hour later, Dr. Mori, his wife and I were seated on tatami mats, sharing a rich green tea with a strong, bitter taste. The rude nervousness that I had sensed from the doctor earlier was now replaced with a certain kindness and excessive concern for my well-being. Mrs. Mori had explained to him that the kasha had attacked me and he now saw in me a kindred spirit. We shared a common enemy.

"When I first saw you, I thought you were her friend," he explained in perfect English. "Another one of the men that she was using to satisfy her desires and then throwing away. Tomoko had been one of my fondest students. I had been tutoring her in English when Aase returned from Denmark. She took one look at Tomoko's young man and put her designs upon him. She even lied about her age just so she could go to the University of Hawaii and seduce Uemoto-san and whomever else she desired. It drove Tomoko to the edge of sanity. Imagine, Mr. McDougal, your own sister doing such a thing to you. Then the news about the young man's death."

"What killed him, Dr. Mori?" I asked. "I'm having one helluva time accepting this kasha bit."

"My wife, Mr. McDougal, is an odaisan. Perhaps in America you dismiss them as spiritual healers or quacks, but in my country they are quite popular and widely believed in. I've been medically trained at the University of California, sir, but there are things I have seen my wife do that I must accept as miracle. She recognized that the Uemoto boy had been killed by what in folklore we call kasha, the corpse-consuming monster. An unseen force of destruction that rends human beings apart as easily as I can crush this senbei tea cracker. To protect us all, she has been burning incense and praying. She covered poor Tomoko in Buddhist sutra and provided her with the prayers required to keep this entity away. Unfortunately, the spell for some reason failed."

"That was my fault, I'm afraid. I interrupted."

"And now it wants you. Here, Mr. McDougal, my wife prepared this for you."

He handed me a small, red, cloth pouch which was embroidered with those oriental doodles and attached to a long cord.

"This is an omori, a good luck amulet. There is a powerful sutra written inside on parchment. Keep this around your neck at all times."

"It'll go nice with my lucky silver dollar." I slipped my dollar in the omori, and put the good luck pouch around my neck. I figured it was the polite thing to do and, anyways, it wouldn't hurt to use all the luck I could get.

"What I want to know is, who is sending this thing after us? Aase?"

"It is hard to believe that she would do this to her own lover and sister. On the other hand, perhaps she is even more evil than I imagined."

"Kasha can be sent," Mrs. Mori added in very broken English. "Abunai."

"Be careful, Mr. McDougal," added Dr. Mori. "Whoever wanted Tomoko dead, wants us dead. I'm certain of it."

Since Aase hadn't shown up since the death of her sister, she remained my one and only suspect. The only hint I had of where to find her was from what Mrs. Cummins had said about meeting her mysterious Japanese lover once a week at a Halawa Heights teahouse. That had to be Kawaroku's. I figured it wouldn't hurt to stake the place out, especially during those long, romantic afternoons when the lovers were supposed to sip tea together and watch the sunset.

I must have consumed a thousand tons of tea and senbei and watched ships going endlessly in and out of Pearl Harbor when, two days later, bingo! The Danish cookie and Japanese mystery man appeared. God bless, Mrs. Cummins.

"Mind if I join you?"

He took one look a me and flung the table he was seated behind across my chest and ran for the exit. Aase let out a muffled scream and tossed herself on top of the table, trying to prevent me from getting up.

"The son of a . . ." I yelled and, rolling out from underneath Aase and the table, grabbed her up by the wrist and pulled her down to my borrowed roadster just in time to see the mystery man pulling out of the lot, racing down Halawa Heights. She struggled with me as I yanked her into Kats' car and squealed rubber as I hit the gas.

I kept him in my sights until he finally slowed down in front of the Japanese Consulate on Nuuanu Avenue and turned into the driveway behind large steel doors that barred me from entering. Her boyfriend must have been a member of the Japanese delegation, but she wasn't letting on to none of it. This was one cold, silent number. All she'd say was that "it was none of my business."

"I suppose it was none of my business that I was almost killed the night your sister was tore apart?"

"What are you talking about?"

"You don't know? The papers in this town are plastered with the news."

"I don't read the newspapers. Has something happened to my sister?"

"She ended up like Shingo. Seems like someone gets close to you and they end up wallpaper."

I didn't say that very nice and she took it even worse. For the last few days, she explained, she had been with her "friend" at the Japanese Consulate. She hadn't heard about her sister's death and couldn't imagine who would want her dead. Mr. Otsuka had become her lover a few months ago. Yes, she was wrong for cheating on Shingo. She couldn't help herself, she explained.

"Since I was a little girl, Mr. McDougal," she went on curling the words with those great lips. "I had been shuttled from one school to the next, from one country to the next. I learned how weak powerful men could become in the presence of a woman. It has unfortunately become an addiction to me, to seduce men who I see as having power. Shingo, on the other hand, I truly loved. I really hoped that he would change my life. I could confide in him. When he found out about Mr. Otsuka, I'm afraid he became outraged and confronted him. I don't know what they said to one another, but then Shingo was dead. And now my sister is dead. It must be my fault, but I don't know why."

She was now sobbing violently, so I nestled her in my right arm and drove her over to Dr. Mori, who gave her a sedative which put her to sleep. Since the sun had gone down, I thought I'd pay a little unannounced visit to Mr. Otsuka at the Japanese Consulate, using the back door, of course. Since the Waikahalulu Stream runs past most of the houses on lower Nuuanu, I climbed along the stream bed boulders until I was at the consulate fence, which I quietly scaled. It didn't take long to sneak up to one of the lanai glass doors, where a furious argument was going on inside between two gents who looked ready to kill one another. I recognized Otsuka right off. He was being berated by an older, more authoritative fellow in a torrent of lingo that was unintelligible to me. Then Otsuka abruptly left, going to a nearby alcove, where he immediately took off his Western clothes and wrapped himself in a kimono. He then sat before an altar that resembled the one used by Tomoko and Mrs. Mori. The lights in the room were extinguished, except for a single candle burning inside the altar.

Otsuka's chanting was deeper and more sinister than that which had been uttered by either of the women. His body began to sway as the intensity of the monotonous tone reached a fevered pitch and a sudden gust of wind blew out the sole candle, plunging everything into darkness. As he continued with his frantic prayers, I felt a clamminess in the air, as if the humidity had just increased tenfold. The kasha enveloped me from behind, pushing me up against the glass doors and plunging me head-long into the room where Otsuka was chanting. In the burst of glass and splintering wood, the chanting suddenly stopped and Otsuka turned towards me, his face twisted in demonic rage. He had been calling for the beast to destroy me, not knowing that I was just outside his door, ready to make an unannounced visit. He leaped in the darkness for something and suddenly a shot went off, slightly stinging my shoulder. The next shot went wild, as I rolled on the floor trying to find cover behind something solid and fumbling for my revolver.

"Yoshikawa-san," a man screamed at the door, kicking it open and letting loose with a few rounds from an automatic. I shot at the bright bursts of light and heard a loud thud as the man fell hard onto the floor. I figured this was my chance, and I scurried out the way I came in, when the point-blank aim from a German luger fifteen feet away stopped me dead in my tracks.

"You meddled, like the boy and her sister. No one needed to get hurt, now you too will have to die."

"You killed them?"

"Kasha did the killing. I only prayed. It was safer that way."

"Why?"

"We all have our assignments. I have mine. The woman gave me cover, but she proved to be more trouble than she was worth. First, her prying boyfriend and then her insane sister. And now an American gumshoe. Sayonara."

The bullet hit me directly in the chest, tossing me back onto the grass outside like one of those ducks that flip over at the fairground shooting gallery. Thank goodness he didn't walk over to give me the coup de grace between the eyes, but called for one of the servants to dispose of me. That gave me enough time to catch my breath and crawl over the fence and hide along the Waikahalulu Stream while I heard an army of men looking for my body on the consulate grounds. Not bad for a dead man.

MacIntosh told me he couldn't do anything about it. The consulate was a foreign country, he said and, anyway, what in the hell was I doing sneaking about in the bushes? What proof did I have that this Otsuka had committed two murders through voo-doo? How do you pin a murder rap on a guy who sits in front of an altar and chants? The deaths of Shingo and Tomoko, as far as the Honolulu Police Department was concerned, would be listed under strange, accidental deaths. Haven't you heard of spontaneous combustion, McDougal? This was something like that, only spontaneous bodily explosion. Bizarre, sure. But in this town, there are always plenty of odd things running around.

The Feds wouldn't listen to me, either. A private gumshoe is last on their roster of credible witnesses. With the world being set afire by lunatics and Nazis, they told me, the last thing they were worried about was supernatural killers.

I kept an eye on the consulate for a few weeks afterwards, but I never saw Otsuka leave. They must have buried the fellow I shot somewhere on the grounds. In November, I accompanied Aase Tsutsui to Aloha Tower, where she was catching the steamer home to Tokyo. Her father insisted that she return to her country, as the relations with the United States continued to deteriorate. I never bothered telling her what Otsuka had told me that night. She may have been a promiscuous two-timer, but even soiled women can have a soft heart. She didn't need to know that her lover was using her for something that he was willing to kill for.

Dr. and Mrs. Mori were there with leis and Professor Cummins even showed up—with his wife in tow. As the ship pulled away, she seemed to be saying something to me and tossed me a message that missed the dock and floated into the harbor. Some nights I stay awake imagining what it may have said, dreaming of the sakura blooming along the Sumida River and Art McDougal chasing windmills in Denmark.

Saturday afternoon, December 6, 1941, I came out of the Kress Building on Fort Street, where I was doing a little Christmas shopping, and thought I noticed my mysterious Japanese friend coming out of the RCA telegram offices. I followed him a few blocks, but he evaded me for the last time. I dropped by my office at Fort and Merchant Streets to pick up messages and plopped down at my desk to try and sort it out. Otsuka, Yoshikawa—or whatever his name was—had to be up to something very top secret. So secret, he was using some ancient hocus-pocus to knock off those who were coming close to exposing him.

"Something big," Shingo Uemoto had said. "Something too big." Nazis and the occult, Professor Cummins had said, a very dangerous combination.

I gently fingered the omori that Mrs. Mori had given me, feeling the place where the slug had entered and then dented my lucky silver dollar. Nah, I don't believe in ghosts and poltergeists. The kasha was simply mass hypnosis. But, that Saturday afternoon I did believe in luck. Leaning back in my chair, I felt real, real lucky. With that omori dangling around my neck, what in the world could ever go wrong?

A Calling
Spirit of
Kipapa

A Mystery from the Files of Arthur McDougal
Honolulu International Detective Agency

banshee—in Gaelic folklore, a banshee is a female spirit whose wailing warns of an impending death in a family.

Sirens—in Greek mythology, the Sirens sang melodies so beautiful that sailors passing their rocky island were lured to shipwreck and death.

Kaupe—in Hawaiian mythology, a cannibal dog-man who traditionally lived at Lihue, Oahu, near the central plains of the island.

calling spirit—in any language, big trouble.

Kipapa Gulch has for many years concealed several mysteries of a most unusual nature. The old bridge that spans the ravine along the Kamehameha Highway has been, for example, the scene of many head-on accidents—a result perhaps of the fact that the structure is on the path of nightmarchers who have sometimes appeared in Kipapa carrying torches on their silent, ghostly walk from the mountain to the sea. Many years ago, a security guard who worked for a dairy in the area told me of the night when he heard several persons crying under the bridge. Concerned that perhaps they had been hurt in an accident, he searched out the injured victims, only to discover something of an extraordinary nature living under the bridge. After having enticed him to its remote, dark lair, the beast then chased the guard back to his trailer with taunting delight. Visibly upset as he recounted the occurrence, the security guard would not describe what this creature looked like, except to say that it was huge and shadowy. He had been warned by a spiritual counselor that, by describing the beast, he would invite its return—even to his home!

What had called the security guard to the bushes beneath the bridge that lonely night? What beast lurked in the dark, capable of catching anyone who passed, but perhaps preferring instead to scare them out of their wits? Why do so many people in Hawaii hear their names called from dark, empty rooms or from beneath deserted bridges where no living soul exists? The female banshee wails that waft through Kipapa Gulch call out the omen of death, but is it your life the demon seeks? Late at night, drive alone across the Kipapa bridge, one eye on the road ahead, another on the rearview mirror to see who has joined you in the back seat. Keep one ear open for the call of your name and the other pinned to the mysteries of this ancient land where murder is no stranger.

The monsters were sucking on me like vampires at a blood bank feeding-frenzy, turning somersaults on my forehead, jabbing me with their poisoned snouts and spinning cartwheels across my nostrums. I was fighting them off with everything except garlic and a cross, and would have considered using my Colt .45 if the targets weren't so frustratingly small. Already their venom had gotten into my system, with large, enflamed welts puffing up wherever the flesh was bare. At the rate I was losing the battle, I was thinking of saving the last bullet for myself rather than endure what would be the unbearable *coup de grace*, the endless night of itching.

Mosquitoes, I was once told by an old Hawaiian, had been brought to the Islands back in 1828 by a disgruntled sea captain, who had deposited the larvae of the vicious pest in local waters in retaliation against natives who had outsmarted him in some trade negotiations. It was no doubt an apocryphal story that said more about the intruding, pesky nature of *haoles* than it did about the origin of mosquitoes in Hawaii. The truth of the story, however, didn't matter at that moment—I was thinking all sorts of unholy things about what I'd like to do to that old sea captain as I swatted wildly and futilely at the squadrons of tiny bombardiers.

The trail that led upon the upper ridge of Kipapa Gulch began to be as pesky and hazardous as the insect monsters that bred in the *mauka* banana farms. With only a sliver of moonlight as my guide, I had stumbled and faltered over every stone that lay strewn upon the path. The trail narrowed as it rose higher over the gulch, until it seemed I was doing a high-wire act with no safety net over the Grand Canyon, wearing a blindfold, while being attacked by mosquitoes. A flashlight would have helped, since even in the daylight I'm no Boy Scout. Yet, I didn't want to tip him off that he had a private gumshoe on his tail, even if my swats against my vampire enemy must have been echoing over to Schofield Barracks.

"Shadowing, trailing and locating," my advertisement in the dailies read, "no case too small, none too large. Reasonable rates." I was getting paid about twenty-five dollars a day these days, mostly to shadow adulterous spouses who had decided to get a little piece of action on the side down in Waikiki, either with some boozed-up flapper or golden-brown beach boy. Sure, it was a helluva dirty way to make a living, but being a private investigator in Honolulu wasn't always romantic. Like the rest of the country, the Honolulu International Detective Agency was hit pretty hard by the Great Depression. John Dillinger was doing pretty good for himself taking out interest-free, nonrepayable loans from Midwest banks, but Arthur McDougal was peeping through windows with his little Kodak, documenting sexual urges from one end of town to another. For a former Captain of Detectives unraveling this burg's worst homicides, it was all pretty humiliating.

Now, here I was in the middle of the night, impersonating a mountain goat, following some two-timer in a rendezvous with God knows what? Two days earlier it had all seemed pretty routine—a bright young kid by the name of Clyde Ito had shown up at my office in downtown Honolulu with a crisp, new, twenty-dollar bill as a down payment for my services. You didn't see a twenty too often in mint condition, so if he had asked me to bare my *okole* at a board meeting of Alexander & Baldwin, my only question would have been, "What time is the meeting?" What he actually wanted from me was fortunately more up my line.

"I saw your ad in the newspaper, Mr. McDougal," Clyde explained, "and I need someone shadowed."

"You don't trust your wife?"

"No, no, I'm not married. I'm not actually here for myself, but for my cousin. You see, she is in great trouble, but she is too ashamed to see you on her own. You must understand that it is sometimes hard for us, as Japanese, to admit to anyone, especially a private detective, that our marriage is no good. Unfortunately, I believe she married the wrong man and is now paying the price."

"He cheats on her?"

"More than that, I believe he abuses her. I've seen her sometimes with ugly bruises on her arms. She says it's from banging into cabinet doors. Once I saw her with a black eye."

Clyde was one of those local *nisei*, who usually kept their lips as tight as a sealed *sake* drum, but who once they opened up held nothing back. I couldn't help but like the young man who was fiercely loyal to his cousin, but who was also maybe stepping out-of-line by hiring a private dick to trail her husband.

"If she doesn't want any help, what difference does it make if her husband is proven to be a two-timer? She probably already knows he's unfaithful."

"She won't believe me about him. Anyway, he has her terrified. He has threatened to kill her if she leaves him."

"So, what do you want me to do?"

"Follow him and bring me proof that he's with other women. You take pictures, don't you? If the photographs don't convince her to leave him, I can show the photos to my uncle, her father. He is a very old-fashioned Japanese man who has hated her husband even before they got married. For the sake of the family name, he'll do something to destroy their marriage. Alex won't want those photos going to his boss. He's got a good job with..."

"Whoa, Clyde. I won't be party to extortion. That's a good way for me to lose my license. This Alex may be a cheat and a wife-beater, but extortion is a felony."

"Of course, Mr. McDougal. I'm sorry. It's just that I love my cousin very much. We grew up together in Pearl City and we are like sister and brother. I'd do anything to help her, and right now I feel desperate. I guess you're my last hope. . ."

His voice trailed off as he became teary-eyed and shyly turned his head down into his chest to avoid my hard glare. Guys like that are always trying to prove how tough and manly they are, so I excused myself to get a shot of whiskey while he composed himself. Ever since Prohibition was lifted, I kept my *okolehao* and whiskey out on an open shelf. I poured myself a tall, stiff one.

"Want a drink?" I asked.

"No," he answered, his composure regained.

"You have a picture of your friend Alex?"

He pulled a large wedding photograph out of a manila envelope that was smudged with the red dirt of central Oahu. He was probably a rice or banana farmer, I thought. These days, no matter what education an Oriental may have had, they always ended up farmers. I wondered how many weeks it took him to save up for that crisp, twenty-dollar bill.

"I see why your uncle hated him. Your cousin married a haole, uh?"

"Yeah. A Russian."

Alex Cherem, decked out in a dark suit and white tie, looked about 25 years old in his wedding portrait. Mari, his wife, was in one of those traditional Japanese kimono with the tall headdress that I was told hid the woman's horns. I knew those horns real well—I had been gouged a few times. What else could I say about her, except that Mari Cherem looked as cute as a doll, an expression I had heard a million times used in describing local *wahine* and which said nothing. If she was a doll, then she had become a battered one.

In the next twenty-four hours, with no other cases pending, I learned everything I needed to know about Alex Cherem. He had been born in Czarist Russia before the Bolsheviks turned the country into a worker's paradise without bread and Stalin had paved the Georgian steppes with the corpses of his enemies and plenty of his friends. When he was 10 years old, his father, who had been a peasant farmer in Siberia, was recruited to work on the Hawaiian sugar plantations. With seven sons and four daughters, the Cherem family arrived in the Islands in 1909, but they couldn't adapt to the humid, relentless work of the plantations, so, like most other Russian immigrants, ended up in the tenement camps of Iwilei. His mother died the first year after a bout with influenza, which was made worse by their poverty. One of his older sisters was recruited into one of the cribs of the district's brothels, where she hitched up with a soldier and moved somewhere east of the Rockies. That was a part of the family tree that the proud Russians had tried to prune.

After three years of struggle and poverty, the senior Cherem was finally hired as a stevedore at the harbor where, at the age of 65, he still worked six days a week, twelve hours a day. Alex was the youngest child, so his father had sent him to public school, and he finally graduated from McKinley High School. A tall, muscular, white Russian with a handsome face chiseled from solid granite, Alex had been totally Americanized in his schooling, losing even the last traces of his childhood foreign accent. He even earned a name for himself playing high school football and was one of Scotty Shuman's fastest running backs on the Town Team.

Women had never been a problem for Alex Cherem—he played them as deftly as he did the pigskin. Mari and he had met during their senior year at McKinley, and, although interracial dating was not approved of by either family, the forbidden fruit eventually ripened into marriage. Alex's father, who didn't want "no mongoloid grandchildren," had threatened disinheritance, but since he had little to leave his son, it was an empty threat. Mari's father equally despised Alex, but his love for his only daughter was greater than his old world pride. A widower who had lost his beloved wife during the birth of their second, still-born child, Koji Hoshino acquiesced to the marriage only on the condition that his daughter wear the *kimono* in which her mother had been married. The happy couple of Russian and Japanese ancestry had been photographed in their wedding clothes at Go's Photography Studio in Moiliili.

The forbidden fruit quickly turned stale after the first year of marriage. Alex found a clerk position with the Honolulu Trust

Co. and, with his good looks, quick wit, and charm moved his way up into the vice presidency of the city's second largest financial institution. He was a member of the lily-white Pacific Club, where he never took his Oriental wife and bragged about his friendships with the island aristocracy with whom he hobnobbed. In the days of "soft-drink parlors," or "speakeasies" as they called them on the mainland, he was also chummy with Duck Pong, the Godfather of Chinatown's rackets. He was never without a platinum blonde on his arm, an Havana between his lips, or a five-dollar tip for the *maitre de*. Yet, like Jekyll and Hyde, he moved between the world of respectability and the demi-monde of the parlors with graceful ease, never letting scandal taint the facade of his success. As for Mari, when she complained too much of his late night hours, he got drunk, beat her, and then bedded her down. He was never sure if she was an exotic pet or a ball-and-chain about his feet.

For the last six weeks, however, Alex Cherem was risking everything for a dark-haired, blue-eyed, white-skinned beauty who had registered at the Halekulani Hotel under the name of "Natalie Dubetsky." Traveling with Polish passports, she and her uncle, "Leo Dubetsky," had taken two rooms at the modest Waikiki hotel while they enjoyed an extended stay in the Islands. The *Advertiser* had described them as "aristocrats who had been dethroned following the Bolshevik uprising." I had only seen her once, holding hands with Alex inside a cabana set back from the beach. His other hand made a great photograph, groping for some luscious curves that should have been labeled with "warning" signs. In public, Alex Cherem was making a complete fool out of himself, waltzing the Russian bombshell in and out nightclubs and the Alexander Young Hotel as if in this little town nobody knew everyone else's business. Clyde could have saved his dough—he didn't need a private detective to discover this slimy little indiscretion which was becoming the talk of Waikiki.

That's why I thought it was pretty odd this evening when Alex left Natalie's room at about ten o'clock and tooled his machine out of town, heading *ewa* through the sugar cane fields of Pearl City and Waipahu, along the Kamehameha-Schofield Highway. Did he have another woman stashed in Haleiwa that even

Natalie didn't know about? I tried to keep a pretty safe distance from his Oldsmobile, lest he see my headlights tailing him. After all, who in the world would be out here at this time of night? We were the only automobiles winding our way across the belly of Oahu, when Alex's car pulled over just past the new Franklin Delano Roosevelt bridge that spanned Kipapa Gulch.

The territory had just had a gala party last April to dedicate the new bridge, which was a concrete beauty standing seventy feet high above the gulch that in years past had claimed so many lives. Before the bridge was erected, getting across Kipapa meant navigating twenty-six hairpin curves on a steep slope. Young kids used to run their machines through the gulch at breakneck speeds, and the toll of the dead at that place was as long as a Castle and Cooke payroll. The bridge was started a year ago, just after FDR's inauguration in '33, and, with the new president's permission, was named in his honor. The American Brewery Company supplied all the free beer you could consume at the dedication ceremonies.

Under the evening's faint moonglow, the Roosevelt bridge now seemed awfully lonely—spanning this gulch so empty of signs of human life. Down the valley, towards Pearl Harbor, I could see the yellow lanterns glowing from the few shacks occupied by Kipapa's banana farmers. Otherwise, the gulch was deadly still, with only the occasional rustling of a banana stalk that disturbed the quiet of this tomb. Cherem had driven off the highway on the Wahiawa side of the bridge, where a narrow, dirt road wound to the floor of the valley. There, finally, he was forced to continue on foot. He had come prepared with a flashlight, which made his hike a lot safer than mine, as I kept a safe distance and moved stealthily in the dark. As I fought the mosquitoes and stumbled through the minefield of ankle-breaking rocks, I kept wondering how a simple case of shadowing an adulterer could have taken me so far afield from sordid sheets. I was contemplating this detective's conundrum when I heard voices far up the trail. He was having a rendezvous with a woman after all.

"Alex," I heard her say, a gentle feminine voice that carried down the valley as if in the wind. I was too far away to hear his answer, but I could hear her sweet, loving laughter in response. A sharp curve in the trail ahead obstructed my view of them, but from the noises they were now making there was no doubt that they were very happy to have found each other. It was a peculiar place for a sexual tryst, I concluded, but this guy Alex had active hormones. The voices moved away from me, walking further up the switchback trail, seemingly rising high above me. Considering the fact that I wasn't a voyeur, I decided that it would be best if I turned back to let the Russian have his Kipapa peccadillo at the top of the ridge.

I was sucking on a swig from my whiskey-filled flask, imitating one of the vampires at my throat and getting ready for my descent when, suddenly, a banshee shrill sent the hairs running up the back of my neck. It was an ungodly scream that came rushing down on me from above. Plummeting head-over-heels along the face of the steep ridge, a flaying leg slapped me across the back, with groping hands struggling to catch any lifeline. I was also thrown off the narrow trail, but fortunately landed in some prickly brush that clung tenaciously to the slope. The falling figure was plunging down the ridge so fast, it yanked the roots out of the earth, causing a small avalanche of rock, dirt and foliage to follow in its wake. The terror-struck eyes of the Russian Romeo passed by me, perhaps surprised by my presence, but more concerned about the boulder at the bottom of the stream bed that was rushing up to kiss him. It was love at first sight as flesh met rock, and Alex Cherem's brains were spilled in a lovely radial pattern across the red earth of Kipapa.

It must have been a sight—a middle-aged, overweight, private gumshoe hanging for his life onto the side of Kipapa Gulch, trying to get his footing, while the sound of Cherem's date giggling now filled the valley. Her laughter sounded more like pleasure than fear, as if maybe she had pushed the poor boob over the edge. By the time I got myself turned right-side-up and, panting, reached the place where the laughter had been coming from, she was gone. By that time, I knew that even a one-legged man would have had plenty of opportunity to have either continued up the valley trail, hiding in one of the many caves, or to have gone over the ridge. Not being a hero, I figured this was now a case for the police.

The next afternoon, I was making out my report on what had happened to Sergeant Henry Chillingworth of the Honolulu Police Department. I kept my involvement in all this pretty hush-hush, except to say that I had been asked to tail Cherem for possible adulterous activity. Captain of Detectives Johnny McIntosh grilled me on the description of the woman that Alex Cherem had met on the Kipapa ridge. I told him a thousand times I hadn't seen her—she had always been beyond or above me, out of sight. By her voice I guessed she was a young woman, otherwise I knew nothing. No, I didn't think she knew that I had been there—I had been pretty careful not to tip my hand. No, I had no idea why they would have met out at Kipapa when there was plenty of hotel rooms in town. The medical examiner confirmed that Cherem's brain had been smashed when he hit the boulder. McIntosh agreed with me that for the sake of the dead guy's wife and Honolulu Trust, it was best to simply say that he died in a fall. At least until the cops had some hard evidence and a suspect, there was no point in embarrassing the living.

When I finally got back to my office, nursing post-traumatic mosquito bite wounds and a sore *okole* from my nesting in the thorn bush, Clyde Ito was waiting for me to pay off his bill. Usually I have to chase my deadbeat clients down, but Clyde had the balance of my three days investigation in clean, crisp bills placed in a spotless white envelope.

"Thanks, eh, Mr. McDougal," he said, trying to suppress a thin smile. Nobody feels totally good when someone gets their head smashed to smithereens, but, considering the victim, I guess Clyde couldn't be blamed for at least a little grin.

"I guess this sets Mari free, yeah?" I said matter-of-factly.

"The paper says that he had a bad fall last night. Was he pushed?"

"Maybe," I answered. "Your friend Alex certainly had enough women in his past who would have liked to have seen him take that swan dive. Then again, maybe he just slipped."

"Who do you think killed him?"

"If he was killed," I said, "it's none of my business. The police are going to handle it from now on. You just better make sure that your cousin has herself an airtight alibi."

138

"Are you saying. . ."

"I ain't saying nothing," I cut him short. A flush of deep anger turned Clyde's face red. "Hasn't that sonuvabitch put her through enough? He's out with some tramp and gets himself killed, and now Mari's going to be dragged into this?"

"Hold on, Clyde. Adulterous husbands don't usually rendezvous with their wives on lonely mountain tops in the dead of the night. If Mari can confirm her whereabouts last night at about 11:30, she shouldn't have too much to worry about."

"I'm going over to her place right now to help her with the funeral arrangements. It's going to be difficult for her right now, but I know that in time she will see that she's better off without him. And one more thing, Mr. McDougal. For her sake, why don't you rip up those photographs you took? She doesn't need to see them now."

The weeks passed swiftly that summer. Dillinger was still busy in Illinois, and I was spending my time scourging in River Street dives for a rat named Kelson, who liked to call himself the King of Tin Can Alley. A client had been burned in a little financial transaction with Kelson, and I was acting as a collection agency. McIntosh had called me to let me know that since they had found no footprints of any woman along the Kipapa ridge trail, they were at a dead end. Natalie and Mari had been questioned, but neither one of them had been alone that evening. Mari had been visiting with her father in Pearl City Peninsula, where he ran a sampan fishing fleet. After Alex had left her that night, Natalie had wandered down to the House Without a Key, where she drank gin into the wee hours with a coterie of male admirers who were not about to forget any part of her anatomy. It wouldn't be the first case of possible homicide that would sit for years in a dusty H.P.D. file.

I had just about forgotten the name of Alex Cherem when I took a phone call from Mari Cherem, the pretty, abused wife whom I had never met. She seemed pretty distraught, babbling something about her life being in danger and some nonsense about ghosts. I calmed her down as best I could, explaining that if she was seeing spirits, she should call a *kahuna*, not me. Never believe in anything that goes bump in the night, I always say, unless it's holding a pistol. Then it earns my respect. After about fifteen minutes of her pleading, I gave in and agreed to meet with her. To be honest, I was kind of anxious to see her up close and check out her horns for myself.

She was living temporarily with her father at the peninsula. The Pearl City Peninsula had once been a fashionable suburb for Honolulu's leading merchants. Connected to town by the Oahu Railway and Land Company train, the peninsula also sported a hotel, a dance pavilion, and yachting facilities for weekend sails in the lochs at Pearl Harbor. Japanese sampan fishermen had begun to move into the area in the 1920s, as many of the old Victorian homes there were sold off or fell into disrepair. While I had always known that Japanese fishermen were a pretty hardworking group of tuna-grabbers, who eked out a living as best they could with their sampans, Koji Hoshino was far from some poor fisherman. His small fleet of ships supplied a good part of the catch at the Kekaulike fishmarket, and his home was as grand as anything his *haole* predecessors had built in the decades before.

I found Mari relaxing in a lounge chair in her father's backyard, watching the fishing boats and navy ships navigate about each other on the waters of Pearl Harbor. She was still as young and as exotic as she had appeared in her wedding photograph, even though she was dressed in a simple, yellow, chiffon dress—right out of a *Saturday Evening Post* cover. I tried hard to imagine someone hitting her or verbally abusing her. I tried to think up a thousand reasons to cheat on her. Nothing came to mind, except a sinking feeling that I had become too old and too wrinkled to ever love someone that youthful ever again.

"Now, Mrs. Cherem, I tried to tell you on the phone that I don't see how I can help you. I was hired by your cousin to assist the family in determining the nature of some of your husband's business activities. As I told you, I'm not a priest. If you have some kind of problem of a personal nature, I suggest you talk with a doctor or a . . ."

"You were asked by Clyde to investigate my husband's personal habits, Mr. McDougal, not his business. Please, you don't have to hide anything. Clyde has told me everything about what took place. I know everything about Natalie Dubetsky."

Her manner threw me off. I had been led to believe through Clyde that Mari was a sheltered little child who couldn't face reality. Sure, she seemed frightened—her voice had almost seemed desperate on the phone. Yet, as she looked me square in the eye, I knew she also had her feet firmly on the earth.

"So, I don't understand why you called me."

"Do you believe in ghosts, Mr. McDougal?"

"Speaking honestly, no. I may have had some pretty strange things happen to me, but when it was all sorted out, it usually came down to either indigestion, imagination or some weasel stalking me in the night. If the dead come back, it's none of my business."

"I think Alex may have been killed by a calling spirit."

"A calling spirit?"

"A disembodied entity that comes to you night after night, luring you to step towards them or answer their call so that they can take your soul."

"Sure, yeah. Well, that's pretty interesting. I'll remember that. Now, I guess I've got to be going back . . ."

"The police showed me your report. You told them there was a woman's voice calling my husband just before he fell to his death. She called out 'Alex,' is that not correct?"

"Yes, Mrs. Cherem, it was a woman's voice."

"Did you see her?"

"No, they were too far up ahead on the switchbacks. But it was a woman's voice, not a ghost."

"The voice of that woman had been calling my husband several weeks before he fell from that ridge, Mr. McDougal."

"You heard it?"

"No, but he told me about it. It had come into our bedroom, he said, one night while we both had fallen into a deep sleep. Her voice stirred him from his slumber and just simply said, 'Alex.' Since I was a little girl, I've been sensitive to spirits. After the death of my mother, she would often come to me in dreams. You must believe in dreams, Mr. McDougal. That they portend the future and that the spirits of your loved ones can communicate through dreams?"

"Whatever you say."

"I told my husband that he should write down his experiences in a journal—a dream book if you will. As these occurrences take place over time, patterns form and meanings emerge. Unfortunately, I think that the calling spirit must have lured him to his death before he could understand the demonic forces that were tempting him. My husband, you see, could never resist a pretty woman, dead or alive."

"Why are you telling me all this, Mrs. Cherem? If what you are saying is true, you certainly don't think I can do anything for you, do you? You want me to arrest the calling spirit?"

"Two ghosts from my husband's past have returned to me, Mr. McDougal, in very significant ways. In one way, you can assist me. In the other, I'm afraid I must help myself."

It was broad daylight, but talking to her made my skin tingle with goose bumps—not because I believed a word of it, but because you could tell she bought this spiritual crap hook-line-and-sinker.

"Go ahead."

"One ghost is very real. Her name is Natalie Dubetsky. Two days ago she sent me a note suggesting that it would be in my best interest if I could assist her financially to meet some of the debts that she and her uncle have incurred during their stay in the Islands. Evidently, Alex shared some of his more perverse thoughts with her in a few letters that she now wants to make available to me—otherwise they will go to the press. I know that Alex wouldn't care now, but the shame my husband brought to me and my father will unfortunately live after him if I don't settle this matter. I'd like you to handle it for me."

"You want to pay her for the letters?"

"Of course. However, I'm concerned that she'll come back for more money with new letters a month from now. I'll pay her $5,000, which my father is willing to give me, but it must be for all the letters."

"You could save some money and have Clyde make the exchange for you. He'll certainly do what you ask."

"Clyde is a dear boy, but I'm afraid he doesn't have the fortitude needed to handle this woman. At any rate, I've asked Clyde not to intrude into my life again. He went too far when he first contacted you. It was none of his business what happened between Alex and myself.

"He only loved you and was concerned."

"Yes, I know. Too concerned. He's very sweet, but growing up with my aunt and uncle in Kipapa has isolated him from real people. I guess you'd say he's like a country bumpkin."

"Your uncle and aunt have a farm in Kipapa?"

"Yes. My father's sister married my uncle, Genji Ito. They have a banana farm."

"Was your husband going up there that night to see your uncle or Clyde?"

"I have no idea what he was doing up there."

"Well, by the way he acted, I thought he was meeting someone. Could it have been them?"

"My uncle's house is at the mouth of the gulch and is accessible by car. I can't imagine why he'd be hiking back in the mountain if he were meeting them. So, Mr. McDougal, will you or won't you handle Miss Dubetsky?"

I told her I would set up the exchange with her husband's mistress for sometime later that evening. As for the $5,000, I would come back later that night for the money. She gave me an address in Kapahulu where she was going to be that evening with her father's money.

"Before I leave, I must admit you've made me curious about the second ghost. You said that two ghosts of your husband had returned?"

"You just want to make fun of me?"

"No, seriously, you've got me curious. You've seen your husband's spirit?"

She became very still, her voice almost whispering.

"Not exactly. Yet, whatever killed him came to see me at my home in Kapahulu last night. At first I thought it was my husband. It was about three in the morning when the doorbell began ringing over and over, as if someone were they in desperate trouble. I thought at first it was the police, or maybe one of my neighbors. I put on my robe and rushed into the parlor, calling out, 'Who's there? What do you want?'

"'Sweetheart,' I heard my husband's voice say, 'I'm home.'

"I love my husband very much, Mr. McDougal, no matter what Clyde may have told you. He had a sickness, but I was loyal to him. 'Sweetheart, please open the door,' he repeated. His voice was soft and plaintive, loving, like when I first meet him years ago. Tears poured from my eyes as I blurted out, 'You're alive!' and put my hands upon the door knob to let him in.

"'That's it, sweetheart . . . open the door! Open the door!' he said eagerly, as if anxious to get inside my house. 'I can't get in unless you open the door!'

"Something then told me that this wasn't my husband. It sounded like his voice, only he ever called me 'sweetheart.' This was the calling spirit that had once followed him, using his voice to get inside the house. It wanted me to let it in so that I would be killed. I screamed and pulled away from the door and this demon kept calling me to open the door. 'Don't you love me?' it asked repeatedly. The doorbell rang and rang again until, finally defeated, it left. I know it will be back, and if I answer the door, I'll die."

"But it was a man's voice. You said that a woman called him."

"It isn't of this earth, Mr. McDougal. It can be either gender, depending upon its victim."

"Well, keep your door locked," I said patronizingly. This superstitious nonsense was obviously driving this young woman mad.

"Mari," a deep, male voice suddenly rose from behind me, sending me at least two feet off the ground and sending every hair on my head straight up, nearly knocking off my fedora.

"What do you want, father?"

I was still catching my breath, feeling my heart race, when a stout, older, Japanese man with a glare that could sink a ship came up to us, grumbling away in a foreign lingo. His arms were as thick as logs, as if he could catch a marlin in his powerful grip and use its sword as a toothpick. I'd hate to be on this guy's bad side, I thought, as I excused myself and drove back to town.

I finally got hold of Natalie Dubetsky and the arrangements to purchase Alex's love letters. I didn't like paying off blackmailers, and she didn't like dealing with a private gumshoe. She wanted to talk with Mari Cherem, she said, or she threatened to blow the whole thing wide-open. I calmed her down, reassuring her that she would get her money. The exchange was to take place at 11 that night under the banyan tree at the Moana Hotel.

It was 10 o'clock when I drove up to Mari's Kapahulu address and parked in the driveway. As I approached the porch, I drew my Colt out of instinct—I don't like entering a house that has its door ajar, especially when calling spirits were known to pay visits. The interior of the room was cast in darkness, only a console radio's glowing light burned in the room, as the Johnny Noble orchestra played a sweet Hawaiian melody from the studios of KGU.

"Mari," I called out, swinging the door open. There was no answer. I slowly stepped in and stumbled on something that lay across the floor, falling flat on my face. I felt pretty foolish as I rolled over to stare into the open, empty, gaze of Mari Cherem, sprawled lifeless on the floor.

Shooting to my feet, I threw on the lights to discover my exotic, little doll with the spiritual sensitivities lying on her back, her head twisted to the side, and with large, bluish-black bruises about her throat. From the position of her body and the bruises, it was apparent that she had been at the front door when someone came in and broke her neck. Her wide-eyed stare suggested that she had been totally surprised, dying almost as soon as she had opened the door.

The cops would be swarming all over the place in a matter of minutes once I called it in, so I took my own sweet time checking out the house. It was a neat little cottage—a bit more modest than you would expect for a highroller like Alex Cherem. By the sitting chair, Mari had left a slim volume that Alex had started, his "dream book," documenting his experiences with the calling spirit. What the hell, I thought, McIntosh wouldn't have any use for something so esoteric. If the couple was killed by a calling spirit, then I figured I needed to know what I was up against. I slipped the book in my coat pocket and drove back to my office to see if I could add it all up.

Alex's "dream book" was either the delusions of a lunatic or someone with a very active imagination. With Mari dead, nothing else really mattered—not Natalie, the letters, the scandal or the shame. All that mattered to me now was resolving what in the hell had happened to Alex and Mari. Of course, it was none of my business. Just call it professional curiosity. If there were any answers to this calling demon, they would be found at Kipapa Gulch. If he wasn't having a sexual tryst in the woods, than what in the hell was he doing up on that ridge?

I did a wonderful job disguising my voice when I called Sergeant Chillingworth about the dead body in Kapahulu, claiming to be an anonymous informant. He thanked me for the information and told me that he'd see me next Thursday at our monthly poker game. So much for being a ventriloquist. Even if it was past midnight, I figured that now was as good as any to find out where Alex had really been going that night. That trail had to have led somewhere.

It was nearly two o'clock in the morning when I pulled up to the end of the mauka road, underneath the Roosevelt bridge. I wasn't alone. There were two sleek Cadillac touring cars parked nearby, so I drove down under the bridge where my car wouldn't be spotted. The moon was even dimmer than it had been the last time I ventured up this lonely gulch, only this time I had a flashlight. The vampires were feeding again that night, but I was getting more worried about the voices that I heard back in the valley. What was going on at this hour in Kipapa Gulch? If these were the calling spirits, then they must have numbered a half-dozen. I passed the area where Alex had taken the plunge, continuing on along the ridge until I saw a several flashlights up ahead. Dowsing my light, I worked my way up off the trail, crawling on my belly to a promontory where the men below couldn't see me.

"Do as I tell you, Ito, or you'll end up like Cherem."

"You killed Cherem?"

"Sure I did. And I can do the same to you."

They came out of a small cave that was concealed by brush, so that from a distance it blended into the face of Kipapa ridge. There was Duck Pong and a few of his henchmen, pulling along a tiny Japanese man, whose red-stained clothing told me he was one of the banana farmers from the gulch.

"You just keep letting us use your land, you hear me, Ito? Cherem tried to double-cross us and he's dead. You tell anyone

146

about this, and you, your wife and son will join him."

"*Okolehao* okay. I say, sure you use my land for *okolehao*. Now, you say use for opium. No good, that kine. *Pilau*."

"We'll stash what sells, Ito. *Okolehao* is no longer illegal. Anyone can buy it. The soldiers can buy plenty of legal beer and whiskey. Opium they can't buy. Plenty of *kala* from opium. What are you complaining about? Don't we pay you? Your boy tried to steal from us, now he's dead. Don't mess with us, okay? Savvy?"

Ito ran up ahead, leading them down from the trail. As they descended towards the bridge, I crawled back down to the cave, where I counted two score of crates, each one filled with packets of the black, sticky stuff that gave men dreams. Pong traded in hootch when it was illegal, and now he was preying on the soldiers at Schofield with the drug that had long been the scourge of Honolulu. With a large stash in Kipapa, it was easy to keep the troops well supplied through any of the small restaurants or stores that had grown up just off base. It was lonely out in the middle of Paradise for the men in khaki, and consuming opium helped to ease the boredom of life on "the Rock." Cherem was probably on his way to the cave that night to siphon off a little of the profits.

The Cadillacs were long gone by the time I got back to my machine. By tomorrow morning, I figured, McIntosh and Federal agents would be pulling in a handsome haul. After all these years, if we handle it right, Duck Pong would take the fall.

I was just stepping onto the running board of my car when I heard the distinct sound of someone crying, a mournful wail of someone in pain coming from under the bridge. Knowing Duck Pong's reputation for breaking bones, I figured that he had given a little lesson in loyalty to Ito.

"Ito, is that you?" I shined my flashlight under the pillars of the bridge, which already had been covered by the jungle growth of a Hawaiian valley.

"Ito, are you alright?"

I moved carefully toward the sound of the crying, remembering my earlier encounter with a corpse. I did not wish to repeat it with the old Japanese banana farmer.

"Let me know where you are. I'll help you."

147

A bush moved slightly, and I stepped forward, peering into the darkness as a trembling hand held the light into the cavernous blackness beneath the bridge.

It lunged out at me with the spring of a mighty athlete, snapping at my throat and growling deep from its gut. My light swung widely, catching a glimpse of the red, burning eyes of the black creature that now threw me back into the dirt, straddling me with the agility of a man, but salivating and panting like a beast. I reached for my gun as it struck me again, hurling me against my car, and the Colt went flying into the stream bed. Again and again it struck me, moving now like a dark, shadowy phantom, as I turned and ran like hell towards the light of a house three hundred yards down the gulch. My heart was pounding so hard I thought it would break right through my chest, as whatever was chasing me stayed right at my back, its tongue lapping at the hairs on my neck, its powerful form towering over me as I ran. The hot breath of the demon taunted me, as the lights in the distance seemed to float like fireballs, moving further away from me as death embraced me with what seemed a final . . .

When my eyes finally opened, I gasped as a huge, dark face with bright, white eyes peered down over me as I laid sprawled out on the black valley floor of Kipapa. I had never made it to the floating lights. With that damn thing panting at the back of my neck, I had tripped over a boulder in the dried-out river bed, tumbling head-over-heels and striking the side of my head against one of the rocks. As groggy as I was, with a welt on the side of my head swelling to the size of a pumpkin, no salivating beast was going to do me in without taking a few licks. I grabbed a stone and swung it hard . . .

"Hey, bull. Easy, eh? I'm only trying to *kokua*."

The monster turned out to be one of the Hawaiian farmers who lived in the valley. To see his friendly face and big, reassuring smile set back my pulse rate a few hundred points.

"Looks like you took a pretty bad bump on your head. You okay?"

"Yeah, I think I'll live. Did you see that thing? Where did it go?"

He looked puzzled for a moment, then lowered his voice,

mumbling to himself only one word, over and over, "Kaupe."

"What's that?"

"Kaupe. You saw Kaupe?"

"I don't know what I saw. Only it was huge with black fur and sinister red eyes. The thing sat on my back like a cat playing with a mouse, its moist breathe drooling on my neck."

"That's Kaupe, for sure. No doubt, bull."

He helped me to my feet, but my legs were still so wobbly that the old Hawaiian had to be my crutch, leading me to a small, grass-thatched shelter that he apparently called home. After a bowl of freshly pounded poi, some dried *akule,* and a swig of the old man's *okolehao,* I was feeling really native and ready to catch a few winks before the sunrise. Yet, as tired as I was, I needed to know more about this guy named Kaupe, who I figured was one of Duck Pong's henchmen. I asked the Hawaiian where I could find him in the daylight, so that with a Colt in my hand I could stand an even chance.

"You never can find Kaupe in the daytime. He only comes out at night. You don't understand. Kaupe is not a man. He is not of this world."

"This isn't another ghost story, is it?" I had had my fill of supernatural nonsense. Sure that beast was strange, but if it wasn't one of Pong's thugs, then it certainly was some kind of wild pig or dog.

"Kaupe does not live in Kipapa," the old man explained, "but has his home at Lihue, an old name for the land up near Schofield Barracks, off the Kunia Road. He's a cannibal dog-man who chases after human beings. If he so wished, you'd be make right now. Dead. But maybe he was only playing with you."

"Right. Well, he can find a new playmate. Tell me, does this Kaupe disguise his voice as a woman to lure men into the bushes?"

"You heard a woman's voice calling you?"

"No, not me. I heard people crying, though, under the bridge. That's why I went down there when your monster came out at me."

"Kaupe is *akamai,* you can be sure. He does what he needs to do to lure you into his trap."

The Hawaiian's face had a golden glow from the *kukui* lamp

that illuminated his little hut. The *okolehao* felt good as it warmed my throat and eased the pain throbbing at my head. The more I listened to the gentle voice of my storytelling host, the easier it was to accept almost any of his superstitious fancies. You can live around Hawaiians, drink with them, and make love with them—but can a *haole* ever really understand them? I came about as close as I ever have that still night in Kipapa.

"Does Kaupe ever go over to Kapahulu?"

"Hard to say. This part of Oahu is his home. From here over to Makakilo and Mililani I know he roams. But Kapahulu? Why do you ask?"

He listened silently as I started from the beginning, with the night that I watched Alex Cherem plunge down the side of the ravine after having been called by a woman. Cherem's little "dream book," filled with references to a female voice haunting him, was crushed in my coat pocket. The old man slowly thumbed through it as I talked about Mari's death, the opium racket and everything else that came to the mind of a tired, old, private dick that was getting sick and tired of chasing after weasels and two-timers. I guess you'd have to say I spilled my guts to the old gent, as if I had been grilled all night under a hot light and finally babbled like a baby. Over the years, in my line of business, I had become pretty hard-core, suspecting everyone of being a liar. Now, here I was confiding in a complete stranger as if he was my priest, or maybe even my father. It felt good trusting someone in this world again. After I was done with my rantings, he went into a deep meditation, whispering almost to himself.

"The calling spirit, my friend, had attached herself to this Alex Cherem. This is not Kaupe, but something different. I have heard and seen these calling spirits, but cannot tell you why they tempt and hurt the living. They can come to you all of a sudden and then be heard and seen no more. Or they can follow their victims anywhere in the world, until finally they claim the soul that they desire. This Alex Cherem, perhaps his good looks was more powerful than even he thought. He used women without returning love, so, the spirit sought his soul to caress her in the other world.

"When I was a young man, I was lured by one such spirit. I

had been visiting my grandfather in Waiohinu on the island of Hawaii and had been out by myself one day fishing at South Point. I was returning to my grandfather's house on a path I had walked everyday for weeks, when suddenly I heard my name called from behind a bush. When I asked who was there, a beautiful young *wahine* came out from behind the foliage, saying that she had a great desire for me and would I make love with her in the woods.

"Now, I must have been only 14 years old at the time, and I had never been with a girl. Shucks, I thought that God had answered my nightly prayers, so I answered, "Sure," and we went off several hundred yards into the woods, to an open clearing where she said we wouldn't be bothered. As she backed into the vine-covered area, she called me to her, revealing her young breasts and slowly backing into the center of the clearing. Hell, I was so aroused that I could hardly contain myself, so I followed her as she kept calling my name. I was so excited, it never occurred to me to ask her how she knew my name, even though I had never seen her before in my life. Young men in heat, though, don't worry about those little details.

"As I stepped onto the vines, the air suddenly turned so cold that my hair froze on my arms and head. 'It's freezing!' I yelled as she pleaded with me to hurry towards her. With every step I took it became colder and colder until I could not stand it. 'Maybe I ought to go home,' I said, backing away.

"'COME HERE! she angrily screamed as I ran off. Again and again I could hear her calling my name as I fled out of the woods, reaching my grandfather's house completely out of breath. Seeing my state of fear, he asked me what was wrong, and I told him all that had happened with the strange young girl.

"'Turn around and drop your trousers,' grandfather suddenly ordered. Believing that he was going to perform some kind of prayer over me, I did as I was told and received the only licking my kind old grandfather ever gave to me.

"'Let that be a lesson, boy,' he explained. 'Never respond to a voice calling you at your back or your name called by someone you don't know. A Hawaiian doesn't talk to your back—it's not polite—and strangers do not know your name unless they are

151

calling spirits. She did not want your body; she wanted your soul.'

"The next day I took grandfather to the place where I had seen the girl. With a long pole stretched out in front of him, he slowly walked into the clearing, poking the earth through the vines. As he approached the place where the *wahine* was standing, the pole vanished into the earth. Carefully pulling back the vines, an old lava pit was uncovered, directly under the jungle growth that she was standing on. If I had taken a few steps more, I would had fallen twenty feet to my death."

"What was the cold air around the girl?" I asked.

"Grandfather told me it was my *aumakua*, my family spirits, who had protected me from her temptations. Your Alex Cherem wasn't so lucky."

He had other calling spirit stories—the woman at Makapuu beach, the one that haunts at the Nuuanu Pali, the one in the old building at Alakea and Queen Streets—there seemed more ghosts haunting this island than there were bootleggers. All these phantoms mixed up with the *okolehao* to give me a permanent case of chickenskin.

"How does Kaupe figure in with Cherem's death?"

"Kaupe chased you, not Cherem. You and he just stumbled into each other. The calling spirit had nothing to do with the beast of Kipapa."

"How many spirits have you got here?"

"Many, my friend. You see, this valley has a great sadness that is hundreds of years old, long before the *haole* came to these shores. In the old days, the *mo'i*, the king of Oahu was Mailikukahi, a powerful chief who had many rivals, especially on the island of Hawaii. Several chiefs from that island, including Kahikulani, of Puna, Hilo-a-Lakapu, Hilo-a, Hilo-Kapuhi and Punaluu, plotted with Luakoa of Maui to attack Oahu and destroy Mailikukahi. The armies landed at Waikiki, but proceeded up the Ewa lagoon and marched inland. At Waikakalaua, they met Mailikukahi's army and a bloody battle ensued. The fight continued from there to here at Kipapa Gulch. The invaders were thoroughly defeated, and the gulch is said to have been literally paved with their slain corpses. That is how this place got its name."

"Kipapa?"

"'Kipapa' refers to the bodies paving the gulch. The Hawaii chiefs were all slain during the battle, the head of Hilo being cut off and carried in triumph to Honouliuli, where it was stuck up on a pole."

The *kukui* oil had nearly burned out, leaving only a faint glow in the hut. The crisp, cool morning air was still black, although I could sense that the first rays of dawn were but a few moments away. The Hawaiian now leaned towards me intently, his face concerned.

"My *haole* friend, you are like a child with these things you don't understand. You think because you see the evil in the human heart, you know better than others what is real and what is a lie. This evil that you see does exist, but you've become blind to the kindness. The shadowed beasts know your heart, which is why Kaupe came to you tonight. You are drawing the spirits of this valley to you. Be wise enough to know the *pono*."

"Yeah, the *pono* . . ." I lingered off into a comforting, deep sleep with the dark-skinned face of my companion set in that eerie meditation that seemed to connect him to eternal mysteries.

A cannibal *poi* dog was lapping at my face a few hours later, bringing me awake with his slobbering kisses.

"What the . . ."

"Who are you? This land kapu. You no belong."

I was staring down the barrel of a shotgun aimed point blank at my head by a very nervous Genji Ito.

"Hey, put that down, mister."

"I tell Duck Pong okay he keep his *da kine* here. No need to scare me. Now you get out. *Wikiwiki*."

"I ain't with Pong. I'm not going to hurt you. Please put down the gun, okay?"

"What for you doing here?"

With the way he was holding that hardware, I wasn't about to tell him who I was or how I stumbled onto his opium stash. So I did what I do best—I lied.

"Last night my car broke down on the bridge. I pulled it off the road and, thanks to a Hawaiian guy, he let me stay in his hut."

"What hut?"

Yeah, I suddenly realized. What hut? Here I was sleeping on the bare ground. Where was that little grass-thatched shelter, the lamp, the . . .?

"You go now. This my land. *Kapu* to you. Go."

All the way back to town I kept wondering about that old Hawaiian guy. Had I dreamt the whole conversation? Yet, it had seemed so real. Still, there wasn't a trace of a hut or Hawaiian farmer where Ito had found me. "You call the shadowed beasts to you," he had said, "and therefore you must know the pono." I had made my life one endless call to shadowed beasts, and discerning any righteousness or *pono* in any of it seemed as pointless as a plantation worker trying to squeeze a raise out of the "Big Five."

My first stop once I got back to town was the hang-out of one of those beasts whose heart was crusted in evil. Duck Pong could always be found in the morning at the River Street on*sen*, or public baths, where he held court draped in a sopping wet towel with his bare-*okole* hoodlum cohorts. I paid my two-bits and washed myself off before slipping into the boiling hot water that helped to soothe some of my aching joints after a night of playing ring-around-the-rosies with the supernatural.

"You soak long enough, Mac, and maybe it'll wash the gumshoe stench off of you."

Duck Pong spoke English with a perfect British accent that he must have learned in Hong Kong, when he was running opium deliveries under the nose of the colonial authorities. If he hadn't turned into one of Honolulu's most vicious and powerful crime lords, I was sure that with his intelligence and class he'd have made a wonderful *maitre de* at Lau Yee Chai.

"At least my stink washes off, Pong." His men made a move to frisk me, but since I wasn't wearing a stitch of clothing, they quickly backed off.

"Calm down your lap dogs, Pong. I'm clean. And while I'd like to stick around to trade insults with you, I came here just to get a few quick answers. It'll be fast and painless."

"Go on, Mac."

"Why did you tell Ito that you killed Cherem?"

"Maybe because I was telling the truth."

"I was there, Pong, when Cherem died, and believe me, I'd

have known if you were anywhere within a mile. You never touched the Russian that night, so why lie?"

He rose to his feet and waded over to my side of the bath, pouring a bucket of the steaming water over his head and arcing a tiny spout of water from his pursed lips that hit me square between the eyes.

"I love the water when it is scalding, Mac, for even in the most intense pain there is a sensation of pleasure. So, too, it gives me pleasure to take credit for Cherem's death, even though I was deprived of the opportunity to personally inflict the pain upon the swindler. That stupid banana farmer believes I killed him, and that is all that is important. As long as he is frightened of me, then I am happy. He told you what I said? Or was it his meddlesome son?"

I had already assumed that Pong had been boasting about knocking Cherem off, but I needed to hear it from his own lips. "My client's identity is privileged information."

"Well you go back and tell your client this, Mac. If he or his hot-headed son try to double-cross me, I promise that they'll both end up with a bullet through their heads. And that goes for you, too, Mac, if you stick your nose in this and cause me any trouble. You don't want to end up like your partner did, do you?"

I put my fist low and hard into his groin in a fashion which would have lost me points if it were a boxing match. The tub of lard doubled up and I shoved his head fast into the water as he sucked in half the bath water.

"You boys just stay put or your pal here visits his venerable ancestors." I pulled Pong out just before he croaked and sent another blow to his solar plexus. All my anatomy lessons were finally paying off.

"Scum like you stay alive, Pong, so the rest of us can feel like saints. You touch Ito or his son and you are through in this town, hear me? And don't ever mention my partner again, not even under your breath."

Onishi had been gunned down three years ago in a dark Maunakea Street alley. My suspicions had always been that Pong pulled the trigger himself, but I could never prove it. I tossed him back into the hot water like a wet rag and quickly made an exit as his boys fell over themselves trying to be the first one to fawn over their boss.

"I'll kill you, McDougal! Watch your back, you dirty gumshoe. I'll put an ax into it!"

"Yeah, yeah," I said to no one in particular as I backed barefoot out into River Street, still drenching wet from my bath and pulling up my trousers. Ten minutes later, I was at my office in the Interisland Steamship Building on the corner of Fort and Merchant, making my regular anonymous call to Sergeant Chillingworth at H.P.D. I told him where a stash of opium was concealed in Kipapa Gulch, enough dope to get the entire U.S. Army Hawaiian Department having dreams. I think I also mentioned Duck Pong's name a few times. If I was going to get axed by my rival, at least it was going to be for something more serious than a little dunking in the pool.

"By the way, Henry, have you got any information on Mari Cherem's death?" The police investigators should have done a thorough job by now dusting for prints and the like."

"No fingerprints, Mac, but a footprint."

"A footprint?"

"Yeah. On the steps leading up to the front door, they found smudges of footprints made with red mud."

"How big were they? Were they human?"

"What d'ya mean? Of course they were human. A man's shoe, size 8 or 9. What's up, Mac?"

"A man?" I hung up the phone and leaned so far back in my swivel chair that I nearly tipped over backwards. With all the weird things that had been going on, I had bought the "shadowy beast" hook-line-and-sinker. Calling spirits, Kaupe the cannibal dog, and Kipapa Gulch ghosts had gotten hold of me, twisting me this way and that until I forgot I dealt in human passions, not supernatural demons. I was back to what I knew best, simple murder.

My best hunch was to pay a visit to the Dubetskys at Waikiki with the intention of seeing whether Uncle Leo had gathered any red mud on his shoes from the night before. Instead, I found him and his niece trying to slip out of the Halekulani without paying their bill. For a couple of White Russian aristocrats, they both looked pretty proletarian in the manager's office, waiting for the cops to book them as deadbeats.

They could tell me nothing about the death of Mari Cherem. They had waited patiently for me to arrive last night with the money to have been exchanged for the love letters. When I didn't show up, they took a taxi over to Mari's Kapahulu home, only to find the police swarming like gnats about the place. They then returned to Waikiki to plan their escape from their hotel bill. Since Alex had provided Natalie and her uncle with most of their living expenses—most of it skimmed from Pong's opium racket—the two of them were now flat broke. They had hoped to use the love letters as a ticket out of the Islands. Killing Mari would have been akin to killing the goose that was going to lay the golden egg.

I must have driven around Kapiolani Park a dozen times, sorting it all out. Cherem's father could have killed Mari out of pure hatred. He had disapproved of the marriage from the beginning. With his "golden boy" son now dead, the old Russian may have decided to do in the wife. Koji Hoshino seemed an unlikely candidate to have murdered his own daughter, whatever disappointments she may have brought to him. That left Genji Ito or Clyde, unless the calling spirit did her in. Yet she believed in all that supernatural bunk. She'd have never unlocked that door, unless she had a very, very good reason.

It was already ten-thirty in the evening as I pulled my machine onto the grounds of the Ito banana farm. Old man Ito met me on his lanai with his shotgun.

"You again. I told you, my land *kapu*. Go!"

I lifted my hands up high above my head and slowly walked towards him.

"Put the gun away, Mr. Ito. I'm not with Duck Pong. I'm a detective that your son hired. Is Clyde home?"

"Mr. McDougal! What brings you out here at this hour?"

Clyde joined his father on the lanai while his mother peeked out from behind the screen door. They were a nice little Japanese family that had gotten mixed up in some very bad business.

"I've called the police, Clyde, about the opium in the cave. You and your parents are going to need a very good lawyer. If you testify against Pong and Cherem, I'm certain it'll go easier for your father. As for you, son, I'm afraid you may have to hang."

"What are you talking about, Mr. McDougal? I had nothing to do with my father's involvement with Pong. At first, when it was bootleg liquor, he figured it was alright. Everyone drinks *sake*, no? They forced him to use his land to hide the opium. I warned them to leave him alone. I was going to turn them in . . ."

"Is that why you really hired me? To get blackmail on Alex to use to get him to leave your family alone?"

The father came towards me with his finger squeezing the trigger of his big, ugly blaster. I don't know if he understood everything that was being said, but I knew a desperate man when I saw one. I dropped, rolled and pulled out my revolver as he let off two slugs that missed me, but peppered my sedan, busting the radiator. I shot once, winging him in the arm. The wife came out from behind the screen door screaming as Clyde lurched across the porch, attempting to wretch the gun from my hand. I swung the butt of the pistol hard against the side of his head, slightly cracking his skull and knocking him to the ground.

"You've gone crazy! Stop! Mr. McDougal, please! You're killing my family!"

"No, Clyde, you're killing this family just as sure as you killed Mari."

"Me? I loved my cousin! For what reason would I . . ."

"Because you loved her. You loved her maybe in a way you couldn't have her. You grew up together as brother and sister, but you developed a forbidden love. After all, in your mind you were really only cousins. Mari never saw it that way, right? The night before she died she hinted to me that you were going too far trying to break-up her marriage. You hired me not only to get the information to blackmail Alex so as to save your father, but to eventually get Mari, yeah?

"After Alex died and Mari still didn't return your love, you decided that no other man would ever have her again. When you learned how Alex had believed he was being called by a spirit in the days before his death, you decided to set up your cousin with her own calling ghost. That night when she believed Alex had come back from the dead, it was you outside that door, wasn't it?

You had her in such a panic she'd have believed anyone's voice was truly her dead husband's. The night you killed her, you knocked on the door and told her it was you. Of course she trusted you. The only way she would have unlocked that door was if it was someone she totally trusted. When she opened the door, you broke her neck with a single blow, not an unlikely skill for someone who hauls banana stalks all day. You even had me believing that it was a ghost that had killed Mari—only ghosts don't usually leave their red mud footprints from the soil of Kipapa."

The kid broke and ran like a scared rabbit before I could hold him. He made it to his car and tore off into the night, his headlights swirling madly through his father's farm, leading up Kipapa Valley and to the Kamehameha Highway access road. With my radiator now filled with gaping holes, there was no point trying to chase him in my machine. Anyway, where could he go? The police would probably pick him up in the morning, parked along the road somewhere, bawling like a baby. It's pitiful the way that a twisted love can turn a decent boy into a renegade.

I had my back to the Roosevelt bridge when I heard the crash. A ball of fire erupted as Clyde's auto fell seventy long feet and slammed into the valley floor. The moon was full that night, casting a beautiful silver light across Kipapa, now pierced by the explosion of a gas tank and the shredding of metal. The air—once filled with the scent of banana—was now soured by burning rubber and gasoline fumes. Instinctively, I rushed down to the scene of the crash, knowing full well that it was impossible for Clyde to have survived. There was nothing left for me to do but to give the last rites.

The laughter was at first nothing more than a soft wind blowing down the valley, a wind that picked up speed until it was the gleeful cackling of something high above me. The plumes of smoke had momentarily darkened the moon, hiding the bridge in lunar shadows. Briefly, the sky cleared, and there was a beautiful young woman in a flowing white gown looking down from the place in the railing where Clyde's automobile had careened off the bridge. She was looking down on the scene of destruction, laughing a strange, hideous cackle that sent shivers down my spine. My head was bursting from the inside-out as a banshee call pierced the stillness of Kipapa. The wail of death was coming from my own throat as I dropped senseless, exhausted and resigned to the shadowy beasts that haunt my life.

Two hours later, I had recovered from my private little act of hysteria and was with the cops retracing the skid marks on the bridge. For some reason that the police never could determine, Clyde had suddenly skidded to a halt in the middle of the road. Then, losing control, he had smashed through the railing to his death.

"Maybe some animal ran out in front of him and he hit his brakes," reasoned one officer."

"Nah, it was a suicide," concluded another when they learned how he had been exposed as the assassin of his own cousin.

"Shame that he messed up the new bridge," added a motor-cycle cop. "It'll cost plenty to fix."

There was no point in telling them about the young girl I had seen, laughing above the wreckage. They would have thought I was hallucinating. After all, hadn't I been having strange dreams of late?

Ito was charged with possession of two crates of opium and was sent off to Oahu Prison. Since he never squealed on Duck Pong, and there was no way I could link the godfather into the Schofield Barracks rackets, Pong walked free and easy. I'm still looking over my shoulder for the ax. Poor Mrs. Ito cremated her son and interred his ashes at the Japanese cemetery in Wahiawa. She frequently visits his tomb, feeding his hungry soul. Hoshino went on harboring a great hatred for Russians, while old man Cherem never did take a liking to Japanese.

As for me, I picked up where I left off—chasing embezzlers, peeping on adulterers, and feeling awfully dirty in the process. It was about two weeks later, as I nursed a bottle of sweet Canadian whiskey in my office late one night, that I realized no matter how hard I tried, finding the *pono* in people was for priests, not detectives. Then I got to thinking about that old Hawaiian man, missing him something terrible. Going out to Kipapa to look for him was pointless. I was going to stay away from that place for a good long time. The quiet sobbing I then heard was coming from me.

"Don't get maudlin on me, McDougal," I told myself as I locked up the office, turning off the lights and latching the windows. The room was pitch black and empty as I shut the door, when, just inside, I heard a distinct and alluring female voice.
"Arthur . . ."

The mysteries of Kipapa Gulch continue even over the portion crossed by the H-2 freeway. A few years ago, a motorist had a flat tire on the section of the freeway that crosses Kipapa. Suddenly, while changing his tire in the middle of the day, the motorist blacked out. When he came to, he was laying on his back beneath the overpass. What had happened to him? How had he fallen off the bridge while changing his tire? After an investigation, all the police could conclude, the dailies reported, was that some unknown person or persons pulled up quietly behind the tire-changing motorist, and for reasons unknown, threw him off the freeway.

A few weeks later, a couple returning late at night from Waikiki ran out of gasoline near the same overpass. When the young man went to get help, he left his companion locked in the car. He never returned. His body was later found dead on the valley floor of Kipapa. What had happened to him remains unknown.

Kanashibari: An Encounter with a Choking Ghost

There were five of us crammed into the little dormitory elevator that afternoon—the Brisbane, Australian clairvoyant Glennys MacKay and her husband George; Kimo Yamamoto, the manager of the circular Mamane dormitory at the University of Hawaii; his assistant, Fred Akau; and myself. I could have asked Glennys to select the elevator button, but I didn't want to play any games. I hit the button that would take us to the ninth and tenth floor level, where we would have to take a short stairway to either floor. As we waited for the elevator to come to a stop, Glennys produced from her purse two small devices that looked like radio antennae attached by a spring to wooden handles.

"What are those," Kimo asked.

"Aurameters," Glennys nonchalantly answered. "They point out energy fields associated with the presence of spirits. If there are any ghosts in this building, they'll let us know."

Frankly, her aurameters looked like the dowsing sticks you played with as a kid when you pretended to be water witching. I would have felt more comfortable with the "ghostbusting" machines used by Bill Murray.

"Do you feel any spirit presence?" I asked, as Glennys went into a deep concentration.

"Oh, yes, of course. It's just a matter of how intense or unhappy they may be. Perhaps there has been a tragic death in the building?"

"No hints, Glennys. You are on your own with this one."

I wanted to make sure she knew nothing about the dormitory—nothing whatsoever. Since she had just gotten off the plane from Australia and had no knowledge about either the University of Hawaii or the strange occurrences that have plagued the Mamane dormitory over the years, whatever information she would give us would be "clean." In no way could she have had previous information. Whatever she told us would either be from her imagination or the spirits of the beyond.

The elevators stopped and the doors opened. Finally, I took the first step towards facing the *kanashibari* or "choking ghost," who for nearly six months had been calling me, calling me for some unknown reason to encounter the terror that comes in the night.

For nearly 20 years I have heard stories about the "choking ghosts" of Hawaii. Who hasn't?

You're sleeping in your bed at night, when you awake to find something pressing you into the bed. You scream, but no sound comes out. You try to sit up, but your shoulders are pinned. When you roll over, something holds you down as if you are in a powerful vise that is crushing your lungs. The darkened room becomes stifling and oppressive—you're passing out from the lack of oxygen when cold, tingling hands touch your neck, the horror choking out your last dying gasp. And then, just as suddenly as the supernatural terror appeared in your bed, it vanishes. Released from its demonic grip, you sit up with the adrenaline pumping through your heart and an uncontrollable, blood-curdling scream rushing from your lips. You have encountered the "choking ghost," the "terror that comes in the night" or the "tie-down spirit" that has both mystified and horrified the human race from the dawn of time.

Japanese, who have had a long love affair with *obake* and ghost storytelling, have called this special kind of spirit "*kanashibari*." While I had frequently heard about such pressing spirits in the Hawaiian Islands, it wasn't until I was visiting Japan in 1989 that I learned how what was translated for me as the "tie-down ghost" also terrorized modern Japanese. It was a dark night in Izu Peninsula, and I was visiting at the mountain retreat of my friends, the Shimoto family. We were sharing ghost stories when Mr. Shimoto inquired if the people of Hawaii saw many *obake*. I mentioned how frequently I had heard stories about the sensation of being choked in the bed when he nodded his head knowingly.

"*Kanashibari* is what we Japanese call it. It happened to me when I was a young man, so I know how frightening it can be. The spirit ties you down and, just when you think you are going to die, it lets you go. So this is in Hawaii also?" Mr. Shimoto asked.

"Definitely," I answered. I then explained how several fire stations on Oahu are plagued with these choking ghosts. From what fellow "ghostologist" Judi Thompson had told me as long ago as 1983, the Kakaako, Kaimuki, Nuuanu, Puunui, Kalihi and Makiki fire stations all had some kind of *kanashibari*. Also mentioned were some of the dormitories at the University of Hawaii and a number of residential condominiums, where choking ghosts had been known to crawl into the beds of the sleeping innocent.

Sometimes the invisible pressing sensation is accompanied with the sighting of an old woman who appears near the choking victim.

I then told Mr. Shimoto that the first time I remembered hearing a version of this story was in 1977, when an Oregon woman who was attending the University of Hawaii and renting a room in an old home near the corner of Maile Way and University Avenue claimed to me that she had been supernaturally assaulted. At about 2 a.m., she thought a large man had broken into her room and leaped onto her back. He must have weighed at least 250 pounds. When she screamed for help he cupped her mouth and pinned her shoulders to the bed. With this man bouncing on her back, crushing her chest into the bed, the woman knew she was being murdered. Reaching up to pry his fingers off her mouth so she could breathe or scream, she discovered there were no fingers on her mouth. Hysterically she twisted her head into the pillow, turning her gaze from left to right. And that was when she saw an old Hawaiian woman with her head lying next to her on the pillow, only about three inches from her own face. The old woman had crawled into the bed and, when they made eye contact, she began to cackle a high-pitched laughter until she dematerialized and the weight on her back lifted.

"Were you dreaming?" I asked.

"No, Mr. Grant," was her reply. "I swear to you I was wide awake. I'm terrified to go back into that room."

Even though it had been a few days since the assault, the woman was still very visibly shaken. She had definitely seen and felt something.

"It happens this way in Japan, also," Mr. Shimoto added. "I recall a friend of mine who had gone with some friends on a tour to Shikoku. She was staying at an old inn, when one night she began to feel the pressing on her chest. Struggling to get up, she couldn't move. Then, floating right above her, she saw an *obake* with a hideous face that had been unusually stretched.

"'I'll get you . . . I'll get you . . . I'll get you,' the thing growled menacingly. She shut her eyes and prayed as the demon vanished. And my friend ran screaming from the room."

Do these *kanashibari* ever really hurt anyone? Most of the stories I had heard, whether in Hawaii or Japan, seemed to be frightening episodes of paralysis. The sighting of old Hawaiian women or oblong-faced *obake* certainly could provoke a heart attack, but could they actually hurt their victims physically?

The only instance of a "choking ghost" actually committing an act of physical violence came from a Kalihi informant who lives along the mauka portion of the valley stream. A few years ago, her little brother started to get up in the middle of the night and crawl into his mother's bed. "Mommy, my bed is dirty," he would tell her, refusing to go back into his room. However, when they checked his sheets they were very clean and fresh. What in the world could he mean that his bed was "dirty?"

Then one night his father took a nap in the bed. A little after midnight, he awoke to feel bugs crawling all over him. Thousands of what he thought were little spiders covered the sheets, their tingling little legs covering his arms, legs and face. Leaping out of the bed, he threw the sheets off the bed, shaking the bugs off. When he turned on the lights, however, he saw there were absolutely no spiders or any other little creatures crawling on the bed. The sheets were perfectly clean. Was this what his little son

166

had meant when he had said the sheets were "dirty"? Of course it must have been a dream, he reasoned. It certainly wouldn't happen again.

One week later, as he was again sleeping on his son's bed, he felt *kanashibari*. Choked by powerful hands around his throat, he tried to pry the fingers off his neck. Finally, after several agonizing minutes, whatever it was let go of him. He excitedly woke up his wife to tell her about the choking. When his wife examined his throat, she gasped. Around his neck were deep, bloody claw marks. At first they assumed he scratched himself when he tried to pull off the invisible pressing hands. However, when he took off his shirt to apply medicine to the wounds, they discovered that the bloody scratches went all the way around his neck and down his back. It would have been impossible for him to scratch himself in that manner. The husband and the haunted room were blessed the following day by a Shinto priest.

Of course, as frightening as these stories seemed as told one evening in Izu, they were, after all, only stories. As often as I heard of this experience, I had never felt *kanashibari*. Although I was impressed with the international nature of the supernatural phenomenon as found in Hawaii and Japan, the fact that the "choking ghost" always seems to appear during a state of sleep suggested it was more Freudian than parapsychological.

Upon my return to Hawaii in 1990, I even discovered that the boundaries of *kanashibari* stretch well beyond the Pacific. In European medieval traditions, men and women were said to be sexually assaulted by demonic spirits called *succubus* and *incubus*. These satanic forces entered your bed while you slept and sucked your breath out while fondling your helpless body. These demon lovers may have been the inspiration for horror stories and erotic art, but they remained unwanted nocturnal guests on the proportion of your very worst nightmare.

Then a recently published Canadian academic work entitled "The Terror that Comes in the Night: An Experienced-Centered Study of Supernatural Assault Traditions," came to my attention. The author, David J. Hufford, has studied hundreds of personal accounts concerning folklore phenomenon in Canada called *hagging*.

167

What startled me was the similarity of the hagging assaults with the *kanashibari* in Japan and Hawaii. Here were modern Canadians informing the researchers that they were pressed and paralyzed in their beds while an old woman—a hag—materialized in their rooms. The cause of these unnerving "supernatural assaults"? According to Dr. Hufford, there were no similarities in the educational, cultural, socioeconomic, medical, psychological or religious backgrounds of the victims. In other words, the usual explanations affixed to cultural or psychological forces did not seem to apply to what was occurring to these subjects during their waking nightmares.

All horror stories are accumulative. You begin with one minor incident and it connects to another unrelated incident and then another and another, until a definite pattern forms that eventually drags you screaming and crawling towards the abyss. In the midst of my academic research into *kanashibari* during the summer and fall of 1990, little did I realize that these unrelated stories would lead me—nearly a year later—into the Mamane dormitory and a face-off with the choking ghost.

It all started with a visit to the Maui Community College in October 1990, where I delivered a lecture on the supernatural traditions of Hawaii to a group of enthusiastic Kahului students. When the subject of *kanashibari* was discussed, a student volunteered that one of the dormitories near that campus had a choking spirit who disturbed students who spent the night in a certain room.

Being a proud alumnus of UH-Manoa—and certain that Maui didn't have anything our campus didn't have first—I assured the audience that several of the dorms at Manoa were also haunted with choking ghosts. The most famous of these spirits was no doubt the one on the ninth floor of the Mamane circular dormitory. The story goes that one lonely night over a decade ago, a student who was dumped by his girlfriend hanged himself in his closet. Not long after this tragic death, it was claimed that at night men who slept in the room would be choked. On other occasions, the shadow of a man would be seen moving in the closet where the young student had ended his life.

It was a half hour later that I was joined by one of the instructors at Maui Community College. "Glen, what was the name of the student in the closet?" he asked me. I told him, first, that I didn't know the name of the student and, secondly, even if I did, what would it matter? "Look at my arm," he said, showing me a limb covered in small goose bumps. "I've never gotten chickenskin like this. That story you told really frightened me because, if I'm not mistaken, the boy who died in the closet was my good friend in college."

Let me clarify something at this point. While I may hear and tell hundreds of supernatural stories in the course of a month, it is not often that the ghosts in the stories take on flesh and bones. For me, the spirits are usually anonymous entities that walk in and out of my stories for the purpose of giving fright. It seemed a little uncomfortable that the famous Mamane dormitory ghost was now a real person, with friends and family.

I recall feeling an overwhelming sadness as this instructor told me the young man's name, background and the reason he believed the young man ended his life. It would not be appropriate to fully reveal what I was told. Suffice to say that his friend had not committed suicide because he had lost his girlfriend, but because of a deep loneliness that was the result of his being an orphan. Ever since his parents died in a tragic fire when he was only 10 years old, he had never wholly recovered. "I never got to know my real parents," he'd say to his friend. "If they had lived, maybe they would understand me."

It was exactly six hours later that I was in the midst of one of my "Ghosts of Old Honolulu" walking tours that the subject of *kanashibari* came up under the banyan tree near the State Archives. I was describing the choking sensation, with no intention of discussing Mamane dormitory, when one of the tour participants raised his hand. He wanted to contribute a choking ghost story that had happened just a few months ago to his roommate.

"Where did it happen?" I innocently asked.

"At the University of Hawaii," he answered. "I'm a student at the UH."

"Oh," I uncomfortably responded, almost knowing the answer to the next question. "Which dormitory did it happen in?"

"Mamane, on the ninth floor."

"Why don't you tell us what happened," I said, trying to conceal the trembling in my voice. What an interesting coincidence, I thought, feeling the chickenskin on my arm. "Synchronicity" would have been a better word, though I could not have known at the time how swiftly the wheels of fate would move.

"My roommate was choked a few nights when he'd sleep in our dorm room, at least that's what he'd tell us. At first I didn't believe him. Not that he was lying, only I figured he was dreaming it. But it persisted for some time and he was getting pretty frightened to stay alone in the room. One night I came home from classes and it was only about 8 o'clock but he was already asleep. I didn't want him to wake up, but it was too early for me to go to bed, so I dropped in our neighbors' room to talk story and drink a few beers.

"It was nearly 10 o'clock when we heard my roommate scream, 'God damn it! I've had it!' He was slamming the door and throwing furniture around. I ran back to my room and found him raging mad. His eyes were flaming and his face livid. 'Damn you. I'll kill you if you ever pull a stunt like this again!'

"'What are you talking about?' I asked.

"'Your little practical joke nearly gave me a heart attack. Don't ever do it again or I'll get a new roommate. You know I'm frightened of this room,' he answered.

"I tried to reassure him that I was in the room next door for the last two hours and hadn't once come back into our room while he was sleeping. Whatever had frightened him wasn't my doing.

"'What happened?' I asked.

"'Well, I had gone to sleep early because I was pretty tired after a late workout. Then I had a really bizarre dream. Someone was pacing back-and-forth in our closet—at least I could see the dark shadow of someone in the closet. I asked who was there, but he kept walking, sobbing heavily. Finally I told him to come out of the closet and this young guy stepped out. He told me he had some problems and couldn't leave my closet. He asked if I would listen to his problems and I said sure, just as long as he came out of the closet. So he took a chair from my desk, moved it to the head of my bed and sat in it. With tears pouring out of his eyes, his breathing wet with his sobs, he told me his problem. He was looking for his parents but he couldn't find them. It was so sad, I sat up and awoke from the dream.

"'It's only a dream; it's only a dream,' I kept assuring myself. And in the darkness of the room, I looked down towards the head of my bed. And the chair was sitting right at my head just as I had seen it moved to that position in the dream! I swear the chair was at my desk before I went to sleep, but somehow it had been moved. I had figured you had moved it to scare me.'

"We told him that it was impossible for us to have moved the chair to scare him—how could we have known what he was dreaming so as to position the chair in a way to frighten him? It just doesn't make sense. So we went to the manager to find out what was going on and we learned that a student had indeed committed suicide in our closet back sometime in the 1970s."

It was a good story and it was told with some effect. Then I asked him to repeat what his roommate had said was the "problem" the student in the closet had discussed in the dream.

"Something about his parents, looking for his parents."

"Six hours ago," I confided, "I met the friend of the student who died in your closet. He volunteered to me that the reason the young man had been so unhappy before his death was exactly the reason he told your roommate in the dream."

There wasn't anyone on the tour that night who didn't feel the tingle of their hair standing on end as a result of that unique coincidence. Of course, it was nothing like the next night when I was talking about these events on another tour, and someone told me that their sister had once been the girlfriend of the man in the closet. Or the following night when five of his high school classmates from Maui quite coincidentally showed up on the tour. Or three nights after that when his sweetheart from elementary school shared with me that it had been years since she had thought of that tragic young man whose life had ended so abruptly by his own hands.

The "synchronicity" of these events, the fact that they were not coincidences, but a series of planned steps, truly occurred to me two weeks later when a wiseacre on a tour suggested that I go into the Mamane closet. "The way I see it," this joker shouted out, "he's trying to get a message to the great ghost hunter, Glen

Grant. Maybe he wants you in the room!"

Well, everyone joined in the laughter. Only it wasn't funny. I'm a coward, I explained. A dyed-in-the-wool coward who would no more spend the night in a haunted room than shoot myself in the foot. And, anyway, what was I to do? Call the University of Hawaii and invite myself into one of their dormitory rooms on the pretext that it's haunted? They'll think I'm crazy, I persuasively argued.

Then a single hand was slowly raised by a young man on the tour.

"My name is Kimo Yamamoto, Glen," this polite fellow said. "I'm the manager of Mamane dormitory. Any time you want to spend the night, you let me know. Here's my phone number."

Fate had determined; it was useless to fight the stream of events taking me to Mamane Dormitory, Room 923. I couldn't put it off indefinitely; eventually I would need to face the music. Certain conditions, I however rationalized, must be met. First, I'd go into the room only in the daytime. Secondly, I wouldn't go alone—I would need to take a priest or clairvoyant who could make contact with the spirit.

Since I don't attend church and don't know any genuine clairvoyants, I figured I was pretty safe. Nearly six months passed and I was ready to mark this up as an "almost but not quite," when the telephone in my office rang. It was a local woman who was calling to see whether I could take the time to meet an Australian psychic who was going to visit Hawaii for a few weeks starting on May 2. Glennys MacKay, I was told, was used by Brisbane law enforcement officers to locate the body of a murder victim and her murderer. She was one of Australia's best-known natural clairvoyants. I was intrigued, so we set up an appointment for lunch on Friday, May 3.

"Do you think she would mind going somewhere with me after lunch?" I asked.

The die was cast. I called Kimo for a 2 o'clock appointment and I borrowed a tape recorder to preserve any impressions or thoughts the clairvoyant would communicate. After all these years, my first legitimate ghost hunt was about to begin.

As we exited from the elevator, Glennys and her aurameters threw me for a complete loop. Instead of walking to the ninth floor, she took the staircase to the tenth floor! I was very glad that I had told her nothing of what had transpired and refused to correct her little mistakes. If Australia's best clairvoyant—who had a 50-50 chance to select the right floor—had failed, then any subsequent contacts with this Mamane spirit would be equally false or fabricated by her imagination.

I'm certain Kimo and I both shared our disappointment silently when about 10 minutes later, after roaming up and down the 10th floor, Glennys stopped cold in her tracks.

"Oh, my goodness," she said in her rich New Zealand dialect. "I think I've got the wrong floor. I followed the traces of a spirit who had been wandering on this floor several months ago, but he is not here now. No, he seems to be elsewhere." The aurameters twisted back towards the steps.

"I believe something is on the ninth floor."

Up to this point, Glennys MacKay's reputation as a "ghostbuster" appeared to be on shaky ground. In fact, without the silly looking devices in her hands , this Australian clairvoyant in her 50s could have passed for a middle-class, slightly over-protective mother from suburbia. It was hard for me to imagine that since her girlhood in New Zealand, before moving to Australia, she had seen and talked with spirits regularly. You could be discussing with her some absolutely mundane subject such as the traffic when she'll suddenly describe some ancient Hawaiian man who's standing on a street corner, watching us.

Her gifts, she explained, were given to her at birth. Although she had been still-born , several hours later she had miraculously been brought back to life. A heart attack in her 20s again sent her into death, only to be brought back again with even more clairvoyant power. A recent "near death experience" has only reinforced her belief that her time to enter the other world is far off. As a clairvoyant, she has become a "spirit rescuer"—exorcising houses and lives of unwanted, troubled spirits trapped for some reason on this side of the chasm of death.

Always faithful at her side has been her husband George, a giant of a New Zealander with pure white hair and a demeanor as gentle as a koala bear. Although not psychic, George MacKay has assured me that when you hang around Glennys for any amount of time, you'll see and hear things that make the special effects of "Poltergeist" seem puny.

Kimo, his assistant Fred, and I make sure to stay a few feet behind Glennys and George. We want to stay close enough to pick up what she says on the recorder, but not near enough to give her hints through our body language of which room, if any, may be haunted.

Glennys now follows her aurameters into the men's restroom. She is so intent on tracing the ghosts, she forgets that this is a very actively used dormitory. Kimo runs ahead to make sure no students are doing their business. She wanders around the bathroom for quite sometime in deep concentration.

"Is there something in here? Some spirit was here very recently. Is this room disturbed?"

"I don't know," I told her. I had instructed Kimo and Fred not to give her any information whatsoever, no matter what she asks. Until this is over, she tells us everything.

Now she walks out of the bathroom and slowly stalks the ninth floor hallway. There are approximately 20 rooms or so, all of them on the outside of the hall. The aurameters point straight ahead with little or no movement. Then we pass room 923 and the antennae swing wildly and turn, pointing straight at the door. "Oh, my, here's something," Glennys says. "Something very powerful. Two spirits are in my presence. Something in this room, and some young girl coming down the hallway. Here she comes, behind us over there."

Kimo and I take a big step back so that the young girl can step by us unobstructed. Fred's eyes have grown to twice their normal size. "Kimo," he says, "do you know about the girl?"

"No, no girl has died in here."

"She didn't die in the building," Glennys explains. "She died in a car accident. She was a student at the time and has returned to be with young people. What is in this room, however, is quite powerful. Can we go in?"

Kimo takes out his master key and walks to the door. I'm checking the tape recorder to make certain everything is going to be recorded. We have come a long way to this door marked 923. I know something is waiting for us on the other side.

"Oh, damn, I've got the wrong key! This is the key to the Ilima dormitory," Kimo suddenly announces after several unsuccessful attempts to open the door. Fred suggests knocking on the door—some students may be home.

"Is anyone in there," Kimo asks giving the door a few strong raps. "Is anyone home?"

What happened next can only be described as an explosion of excitement, screams and complete confusion that were fortunately preserved on the tape recorder. I've listened to this tape over and over. In my mind I've relived those few agonizing minutes repeatedly. Had my "white crow" flown across the barrier between life and death, revealing the horror and pain that for over 10 years had lived in this single college dormitory?

I've listened over and over to the scream that Glennys emitted, mingled with Kimo's innocent knocking on the door, his calling out to those who may be inside. The gurgled, terrible cry of the clairvoyant who fell dead away to the floor shocked all of us. It was followed by a deeper voice who growled out from the depths of her guts.

"Jesus Christ. I didn't mean to die." It's Glennys voice, but it is devoid of her accent. It's American in tone and manly in resonance. And terrible choking sounds are coming out of her lungs. "Can't breathe," she desperately repeats. The clairvoyant I have brought to room 932, the final step in the long encounter with *kanashibari*, has ended up being pressed to death on the cold floor of Mamane.

The sound on the tape swirl around Glennys' choking and attempts of the spirit to speak through her. Students shouting out of their rooms, "What the hell is going on?" Kimo reassuring them to go back in their rooms. Fred and George trying to help lift Glennys up so she can catch her breath. And finally George's voice above all others beginning a chant to help Glennys in her tortured possession.

"Go into the light," George says over and over. "Go into the light; go into the light."

My trembling hands hold the tape recorder so that we can have this for posterity. Swallowing, I note a burning pain in my throat. Is it strangling me also? I try to swallow my spit, but my neck muscles are so taut, a stinging sensation rushes into my mouth. My God, I think. I've killed Glennys. Her heart is weak and this thing is killing her. It had wanted me—it had called out to me—but it has possessed her and her heart is giving out. "George, what can we do? My God, we've got to get her air."

George ignores me as his chant continues, "Go into the light." Glennys now seems to have recovered her air. She's propped up against the wall trying to tell us something. From the tape and memory, I can reconstruct the following words and sounds:

"I'm standing on a chair. (tortured breathing) Rope or belt around my neck. Ah, God, it is so painful. I jump. (tortured choking) I don't want to die. I changed my mind. (long pause, low chant begins in unrecognized foreign language) Tommy. . . Tommy. . . Tommy. . . (long, deep breath of relaxation, as if whatever has been choking her left)."

In about five minutes, it was over. Glennys didn't die and I didn't faint as I thought I would at one flushed moment. I was so fixated by the thought that I had killed the clairvoyant and that the pain in my throat was the kan*ashibari* moving in on me, I hadn't provided much help to George and Glennys. It took all of us at least 30 minutes to calm down.

"He died by suicide in this room several years ago," Glennys explained to us. "But he was kept in this world by some tragic unhappiness. He hurt people in his confusion, but he was not evil. He was looking for someone. When I held a spiritual light out to the room, he saw it and entered my body. It was this young, powerful man who was speaking through me. I was totally unprepared and I'm afraid I must have given you all a great shock. But I had never before in all my years of clairvoyance ever encountered a spirit so strong."

176

"Is he still here?" Kimo asked.

"No, he found who was looking for him. You see an older couple appeared near us within a tunnel of light. I showed him the light and he left me for them. He is with them now. I believe it is his parents. Were his parents dead?"

Everything I had known about the suicide in room 923, Glennys MacKay had revealed through her exorcism in the hallway that afternoon on May 3. Of course, she may have been reading my mind or it may have been a tremendous coincidence. It would have been impossible for her to have had previous information on Mamane's hauntings or the nature of the suicide in Room 923. If nothing else, it probably was the most exciting moment I had ever had in my quest to find verifiable evidence of a life after death.

Before I release you, dear reader, from this story, there are but a few more dangling threads which perhaps can be tied up.

1. Why had she walked into the men's bathroom and insisted that something was in the facility as recently as two days before? As far as we were concerned, only Room 923 had evidence of a haunting. During the commotion, several students had learned that an "exorcism" was taking place and returned later to meet and talk with Glennys. During the course of the conversation, one of the students invited her to exorcise the spirit in the ninth floor men's bathroom. What spirit?

Exactly two nights earlier, he volunteered, he was brushing his teeth at one of the sinks when he felt a tingle on his shoulder, like someone had placed a hand upon him. No one was in the mirror behind him, but when he looked over at the towel rack, one of the towels was being lifted up by the corner as if by invisible hands. He fled from the room but had not told anyone else lest they think him crazy.

2. During the replay of the tape recording, almost everything is perfectly audible except the chanting of the foreign language and the calling out for "Tommy." Although I vividly remember hearing Glennys chant what she describes as the language of the spirit world, it is not on the tape. Most disturbingly, instead of the name "Tommy" spoken three times, all that recorded was a sound similar to that made by air rushing through clenched teeth.

Glennys informs me that if spirits do not wish to be recorded, they simply will not be recorded. What happens on the recording remains an unsolved mystery.

3. Several weeks after the contact with the spirit in the closet, another strange coincidence took place on one of my downtown tours. For a long time no one had come up to me to say, "Oh, I know that boy," as they had six months earlier. Then in August a couple asked at the end of the tour whether or not they could talk to me. We were in the Kawaiahao graveyard and it was about 9:30 p.m. when the tour had disbanded. They told me that they had known the boy who had committed suicide and his parents. They were touched by the hope that his spirit had found comfort in the other world. Maybe he hadn't sought to hurt me, but for me to serve as the conduit for his rescue. I told them that I hoped that was true. Why should a *kanashibari* necessarily be evil? Maybe it could be simply an unhappy spirit seeking solace.

"By the way, do you know who Tommy is?" they inquired.

"No," I honestly answered. In all of the limited information I had been given, no one had ever mentioned the name Tommy.

"We'd just like you to know, Glen, that Tommy was his closest friend and favorite cousin. We'll let him know that he was given a final farewell before his cousin left this world."

They left me alone that night at the entrance to the old graveyard, which over the last five years I have used so often as a setting for my tours. I've walked among these quiet graves so frequently, I've sometimes forgotten that this soil is filled with the remains of those generations who have gone before. That night, like no other night, I felt that the veil that separates us from our loved ones can be lifted. Yet, as the shroud fell once more upon the dead, a powerful yearning possessed me. If we had indeed done it once, couldn't we make contact again?